'SWEET AS'

Contemporary

Short Stories

by New Zealanders

First published in 2014 by the
Sweet As Short Story Project
Wellington, New Zealand

For copyright details of individual stories see page opposite.

SweetAsShortStories@gmail.com

Cover design © Charlotte Hird

ISBN 978-0-473-29348-2

'Sweet As' Contemporary Short Stories by New Zealanders

My Mother and the UFO © Kate Mahony
The Ring © Linda Bennett
In Bath, in Autumn © Gay Buckingham
You Look Beautiful When You Smile © Celia Coyne
What Anton Learns in the Queue © Janis Freegard
Game Face © Lilla Csorgo
The Fighter © Anahera Gildea
The Leaping Place © Vivienne Joseph
These Last Desires © Wes Lee
Making Room for Music © Vivienne Ball
The Great Balance © Jo Randerson
The Greedy One © Rachel Marr
Shine a Light © David Mason
Death at Twilight © Frances Cherry
Oriental Bay © Rebecca Styles
The Snack Machine © Lawrence Patchett
Green Man © Kay Meyer
Flower, Flowers © Wendy Moore
No Way Back © Janet Nixon
Grandad's Shadow © Margaret Orange
White Sunday © Debbie Newlove
Moonlight Crossing © Deb Potter
Overboard © Blair Polly
Nobody's Wife © B.L. Stocker
Phillip's Face © Holly Painter
Through the Belgian Glass © Maggie Rainey-Smith
Memories: Sweet as Honey, Bitter as Lemons © Kathy Sewell
Sorry? © Paula Slack
How I Found My Father © Brindi Joy

TABLE OF CONTENTS

ACKNOWLEDGMENTS

'The Snack Machine' previously appeared in *I Got His Blood On Me: Frontier Tales* (2012) by Lawrence Patchett, and the editors gratefully acknowledge Victoria University Press for permission to republish this story (vup.victoria.ac.nz).

'How I Found My Father' by Brindi Joy previously appeared in *Takahe 68 Summer 2009* (takahe.org.nz).

'You Look Beautiful When You Smile' by Celia Coyne previously appeared in Penduline Press (pendulinepress.com).

'In Bath, in Autumn' by Gay Buckingham was previously broadcast by Radio New Zealand and they retain the broadcasting rights to it (radionz.co.nz).

'These Last Desires' by Wes Lee was first published in the UK in *The Warwick Review* (the University of Warwick's International Literary journal).

'The Leaping Place' by Vivienne Joseph was first broadcast on Radio New Zealand 2009 (radionz.co.nz).

'Through the Belgian Glass' by Maggie Rainey-Smith was first published by *4th Floor Journal* (4thfloorjournal.co.nz).

'The Great Balance' by Jo Randerson was first published in *Tales from the Netherworld*, Steele Roberts, 2013 (steeleroberts.co.nz).

INTRODUCTION

'Sweet as' is a typically New Zealand term meaning okay, cool, better than good, or even awesome. However, the stories in this collection are not all 'sweet' in the traditional sense. New Zealand is a country of light — both strong and bush-dappled — but it also has a dark side.

These short stories speak to us of the diverse world we live in. They take us on a journey, or offer a glimpse into another's life. Some show the struggles, tough questions, hard times, and challenging situations people face. Some stories are sweet or humorous, while others are quirky or just plain entertaining. All in all, they provide us with a snapshot of life in New Zealand and how New Zealanders experience life overseas.

For this collection, we sought contributions from New Zealand citizens or permanent residents (domiciled in or out of New Zealand). This gives a breadth of story lines; 'sweet as' in their variety and quality. Our aim was to continue one of New Zealand's finest traditions: its strong culture of reading and writing, especially in the area of short fiction. Katherine Mansfield's work is widely known and respected throughout the world and many notable others have followed in her footsteps.

Ironically, while we as a nation may be known for our expertise in writing short stories, it's also true that there are far fewer outlets available to publish those stories. *Sweet As* provides that opportunity and we are pleased to add to the history of short story writing by New Zealanders.

When we began this publishing project, we were excited by its possibilities yet daunted by its complexity. However, our initial apprehension disappeared after our approach to the contributors whose pedigrees you will find in the biographies at the back of this book. Their enthusiastic response was to generously allow us to use their stories, which are the heart of this project. To these authors go our special thanks.

To Charlotte Hird we extend many thanks for her cover design and artwork. Charlotte also donated the original watercolour for auction at the book launch (www.charlotteswebdesign.co.nz).

Thanks to the many supporters who donated their time, advice and professional skills, such as proofreading, formatting and editing, that go into making a project like this a success. They include Susan Belt, Anne Gilbert (IHC), and Maggie Rainey-Smith, Frances Cherry and Vivienne Ball from the New Zealand Society of Authors. Thanks also to Kate Mahony, who offered much useful advice and was the catalyst for the formation of the writing group (Rachel Marr, David Mason, Debbie Newlove, Janet Nixon, and ourselves) that first envisioned 'Sweet As'.

The beneficiary of this project is IHC Wellington. IHC advocates for the rights, inclusion and welfare of all people with intellectual disabilities and supports them to live satisfying lives in the community. It is a membership-based organisation with a strong volunteering element and possesses New Zealand's most important library relating to intellectual disability. We hope the funds raised by this anthology will help in their efforts.

And last but not least, to all of you who have bought this book in support of the IHC, all we can say is, sweet as!

Blair Polly and Wendy Moore
'Sweet As' Project Editors
Wellington, 2014

My Mother and the UFO – Kate Mahony

When I was a child, my mother said she'd seen a UFO and I believed her for a whole morning.

It's different now. I'm the one in charge. I give the wheelchair I've borrowed from the rest home a gentle shove. 'Mum, there's the playground. You used to bring us kids here.'

'Yes.'

'See the swings?'

'Yes.' Her voice is deeper and more faraway since my last visit. She says less. It's hard for her to find the words.

It's possible she doesn't recognise the playground. In the old days, it was tucked behind a big row of trees at the south end of the harbour. Now the trees are gone and the space opened up. I grab the handles of the wheelchair again, take a deep breath and push.

'Off we go,' I say. I break into a jog. I can't see her face. I should ask her my questions now. But even though her body is tiny, my breath becomes jagged with the effort and I can't speak.

The next day, at the motel, I try to persuade Axel to come with me again to see his grandmother. He looks up from his laptop and says he came yesterday, she doesn't know who he is, and he doesn't like the smell. Anyway, she's my mother. He makes it sound like I got him here on false pretences. It's a long speech by Axel's standards.

It's mid-morning by the time I arrive at the home. At the door of the dayroom, I pause for a moment and peer around the line-up of resigned faces. Some are dozing already. It occurs to me I'm always expecting to find a tallish woman with coiffured blonde hair and strikingly blue eyes. A woman with strong features and traces of a Dutch accent. Once long ago in Holland, when she was nineteen,

Mum won a local beauty contest. A newspaper article showed her wearing a tiara. She brought the photo in her suitcase when she came to New Zealand with my father.

Finally I see her in the corner, a small woman with a faraway expression on her face, gazing at nothing. I wave, but she ignores me. Perhaps she doesn't want to accept that this grown woman with glasses and furrowed frown lines could be her daughter. I go over to her. 'Hello, Mum.'

She focuses on me, and there's that same questioning interest I see on the faces of some of the other residents. Then, 'You,' she says. She waggles a finger at me.

'She's been waiting for you,' her neighbour says.

Mum looks up. 'I've been…' Nothing else comes. She waves her hand.

'Waiting for me to arrive?'

She thinks about this. She shakes her head.

'Not waiting for me to arrive?' Where is this going to lead us? 'I'm here now and we can have some fun,' I tell her.

A heavy woman wearing fluffy slippers looks up as if she might be about to appropriate Mum's visitor for herself. They do that, some of these old people.

I tell Mum that I've come to take her out for a drive. I help her get up from the La-Z-Boy and she negotiates her walker so it's exactly where she wants it.

'Off,' says her neighbour.

Mum begins to push forward. She seems eager to leave her neighbour behind as if to say, I'm *her* visitor. But maybe that's not what she's thinking at all. Rather this is me attributing meaning to my mother's facial expressions.

At the doorway, I look back at the quiet line-up of elderly ladies in pastel sweatpants. One of them has chocolate on her mouth and chin. Their walkers in front of their feet, they stare vacantly at the big flat screen television. They've already forgotten us.

Mum sits beside me as I drive. She is so low in the seat that from outside it might seem as if my passenger were a small child. Now and again, her head bobs heavily to one side, as if she's snatching a quick nap. I point things out. 'Look, Mum, man on a tractor. He's holding up the traffic. Making them slow.'

'Yes.' Her voice appears to come from a place of deep sleep.

I draw her attention to other things, just as I had shown Axel when he was a toddler. A fire engine. A police car. 'Look at the old man.' He's riding a mobility scooter.

Mum peers out the window. 'Fat man,' she observes. It's true.

As we near my old secondary school, I feel my throat get dry. I could ask her now, *Why did you never stick up for me?* Instead, I say, 'That's the school'. I find myself braking, and the car comes to a halt. The glass on the window at the end of the building glints. The principal's office. 'That's where Ivan was principal.'

I wonder if she remembers my stepfather, her former husband. It has been years since he died.

Ivan had been in the army. He liked to boast how he'd turned the school around, that the parents supported the hard line he took with the louts. Discipline was key. Perhaps that was why it was so important to him that the family he'd taken on appeared well disciplined. But right from the start, he was always harder on me than my two brothers.

When I was in the fourth form, Ivan told Mum I'd become rebellious. He said I needed straightening out.

The sun strikes the window at the end of the building — Ivan's office — and I'm back in there. After my form teacher sent me to him for talking back in class, Ivan made me wait in that room. He filled in records, chewing his way through a packet of Minties; I sat at a table near the door, and tried to do my biology homework. I heard the sounds of the teachers' cars starting up, heading off for the day.

When Ivan reached around behind me, I thought he was taking the school strap off the hook on the door. Instead, he grabbed my ponytail.

'Right,' he said. 'Come with me.' In the boys' lavatory, he handed me a brush and bucket and indicated one of the cubicles. 'Get this cleaned up.'

I was still inside scrubbing at the mess on the sides of the bowl when I felt his warm fetid breath against my ear. Stale tobacco mixed in with something tangy and sweet. Minties. 'Not good enough,' he said. His hand pushed against my ponytail until my face was an inch away from the waterline.

That evening, I tried to tell Mum when we were alone, but Ivan had got in first.

'Your teachers have been complaining.' She concentrated on peeling a potato. 'Ivan says you've been making up stories. You can't say something without embellishing it.'

'It's not true.' I could feel hot tears swell up beneath my eyelids.

'No? You told me a lie last week.' She said it calmly. Implacably. 'About where you were.'

I sighed. 'That was different.' A group of us girls were supposed to go to the public library in school time to work on our projects. It'd been Jenny Eames' idea to bunk off and go around to her house. We had sat around chatting. The next day when Mum asked me where I'd been, I said, at the library.

'You lied to me about that,' she said. 'You're just like your aunt. She could never tell a story straight. You better learn to speak the truth, girl, because if you don't it's going to cause you a lot of grief in life.'

'I'm not lying, Mum,' I said.

I notice even now, sitting here with Mum in the car, I'm shivering. I don't expect her to say anything and am surprised when she does: 'No kids.'

The playground is empty.

'They're in school now,' I tell her. 'Doing their work.'

She seems relieved. 'Good.'

Ivan liked to say that he was old-fashioned. Not surprising since he and Mum met at a hardline church that had only a handful of members. He didn't approve of anything. When I got my first bra, he noticed and said I was thrusting out of it. He'd say it to me when he came up behind me in the stationery room next to his office, his breath warm against my ear. And always that sharp whiff of Minties.

I couldn't find the right words to tell Mum about any of this. When I tried to say he made me feel funny, I saw her face harden. She stared resolutely out the window. 'It's going to rain,' she said. 'Bring the washing in.'

When I think about it now, I'm proud that it's so different between Axel and me, the talking, I mean. He says what he thinks. He wouldn't let me get away with ignoring something. I think about telling Mum how proud I am of Axel, how everything has worked out well with just the two of us even though when I had him I was the oldest mother in the maternity ward. I would've liked to have settled down with someone, but I never had much luck in that department. I'd had dates tell me I was too cold. Remote. Unemotional.

We stop at a quiet café and Mum scoffs the scones with their clots of cream and home-made strawberry jam. The lady behind the counter makes a fuss, and takes a small chocolate egg out of a glass jar and hands it to her.

Mum tries to undo the shiny wrapping on the chocolate egg. Her hands shake these days, but I leave her to it; it's something to occupy her. I'd prefer the café to be busier so we'd have things to remark on, something that can pass as conversation. But then Mum looks up and says, urgently, 'We should go'.

So we go.

At the rest home, I take Mum to her room. When Axel saw it on our first day in this town, he said it was like a prison cell.

If she'd come to Auckland, I could've put her in one of those brand new places with the five-star treatment and the atriums and cinemas and bowling alleys. But she'd wanted to stay in her own home and when the time came for decisions on her behalf, my brothers chose here. She knew people. They knew her. I let them decide.

We'd spent a weekend, my brothers and I, sorting through her stuff. As I'd carried boxes out to the car, to take to the home, one dropped and came down hard on the concrete. When I opened it, I saw that the glass in Mum and Ivan's wedding photo had smashed. There was Mum in her good suit — no wedding dress; it was after all a second marriage, she'd been a widow for less than a year. Ivan stood tall, black hair slicked into place with grease. I peered at the glass fragments, remembering the coldness of his smile. The photo was ruined. Not worth taking it to the home now. That's what I said to the others.

I've never told them about Ivan.

My little brother, Raymond, even seemed to like him. Our stepfather went on Scout camp as a parent helper. He told lame jokes to the kids around the campfire at night, Raymond said, but he said it like it was something good about him. He'd also got in the river when it was freezing cold and helped carry the smaller kids across so they didn't get wet; one of them being Raymond, of course. Raymond must've got Pollyanna genes. He was a cute-looking kid and always had a big smile on his face — some of his friends call him 'Smiley' to this day — and he knew how to get around people. Maybe it was just that he wasn't a threat to Ivan.

When Raymond got married he chose a girl from the church, a round-cheeked kind of girl with the same sanguine nature as his. Between them, they do a lot of buoyant smiling and praising the Lord which doesn't leave much room for reminiscing about the past. I get the impression he doesn't really want to know anything anyway. It would make it awkward for him and his chirpy wife, them with their roles in the church pastoral team and all that.

Tom, our elder brother, simply doesn't like anything emotional or that might involve him hearing something he'd be forced to act on. When the manager at the retirement home gave him the pamphlets on Dementia and Alzheimer's and Other Related Illnesses, he barely glanced at them. After we trooped out of her office and I was spraying hand sanitiser onto my hands near the front entrance, I saw him shove them straight into a rubbish bin.

Now I help Mum out of her coat, unwind her scarf from her neck.

'No one ever wants to know,' I say aloud.

'No,' Mum says. She sneaks a half look at me. 'No.' She says it again in a stronger tone. I almost expect her to add, 'You're right there!' Except, of course, all she is doing is waiting patiently for me to tell her what to do next.

'I'll bring Axel next time.' I'm not sure how I can force an almost 18 year old to do anything, but there must be something I can bribe him with.

'Little girl.' That's what Mum says when I turn up at the dayroom with Axel just after lunchtime. He'd slept till noon and then it had taken a lot of persuasion — of the financial kind — to get him to come. But I'd persisted. I knew I couldn't face another visit with Mum on my own.

'No, this is Axel,' I say.

Mum looks at me as if I were crazy. 'Little girl.'

There are no other visitors. Perhaps there was a child here earlier.

'Lost.' She's ignoring Axel. I don't know whether to be offended or not, especially after all the effort of dragging him here. I can see that he's pinching his nose with his fingers so he won't have to inhale the stinky hospital smell.

'She's probably gone home with her mother,' I tell her.

'Yes,' Mum says.

In the car, I turn the key in the ignition and try to think where we can go. There's not that many places to see around here. You see them once and that's it. I drive out of town towards the bridge.

When I stop the car, I turn back to look at Axel. He's texting, head down, as if he couldn't care less about what there might be to see. And why should he? I've told him I hated this town. I never wanted to go back there. But now I want to get his attention, tell him

17

what Mum saw, even though I never really believed her about it anyway. It's something to do with all those computer games he plays. I want to impress him.

'See over there?' I say.

Axel grunts.

'That bridge.' I know Axel barely listens to anything I say, most of the time. He glances up from his phone, follows where I am pointing. 'That's where your grandma reckoned she saw a UFO.'

He checks out the window. He looks back at me. Half annoyed. 'Yeah,' he says, like I've wasted his time.

Now I am annoyed. 'Yeah.' I mock his tone. 'Early one morning back in the 60s.'

I turn away and look at Mum peering out the window. I tell the story conversationally as if she might be able to follow it. 'You'd been cleaning the church. You came racing in to the house and told us that you'd seen something with lights — like a ring of diamonds — in the sky.'

'Yes.' Mum seems to be listening. Taking it in.

'It hovered above the overbridge. It was bright and scary. You were frightened. You were scared to stop the car and so you drove home, terrified.'

Axel doesn't say anything. Nor does Mum.

Then I feel guilty about bringing it up — just to outsmart Axel — because I remember what happened afterwards, Mum turning on the radio hoping for news, and us all hopeful and pleased for her. She drove back later that day, taking us kids, saying there must surely be brown scorch marks on the ground, the lights had been so strong. Raymond pretty soon got bored when there was nothing to see. Then the day passed and there was no mention of the sighting on the radio, nor anything in the newspaper the next day. I'm not proud of this, but I even sided with Ivan over it: Tom and I laughed at Mum for imagining such a thing and when Ivan said she was just being silly, we nodded our heads. Mum didn't mention it again.

'But there never was anything about it in the newspaper,' I say out loud, half to myself. 'Never.'

I start up the car and drive off. There must be somewhere else we can drive by to occupy the time.

Axel refuses to get out of bed the next morning when I want to visit the rest home. He says he will stay at the motel. He will keep himself amused. So it's just me again when Mum looks up from her seat in the dayroom. She flaps her hands in frustration. 'Little girl.' She can barely get the words out. She says it again.

The manager at the home told me about this another time. The way elderly people can become agitated. It's one of the things to do with Alzheimer's. For many, the agitation comes on in the evenings. 'There's a name for this. We call them the sundowners.'

A young Filipina nurse aide is pushing a woman in a wheelchair over to a table piled high with boxes of ancient jigsaw puzzles. 'Excuse me,' she says. 'You know, I think she might mean the little girl who has gone missing in Christchurch, the three-year-old. It's all over the news again this morning. They've searched everywhere.' She points to Sky News playing on the oversized TV screen.

I remember seeing it on the news a few days ago. A little girl playing in the yard while her mother turned her back to hang out the washing. Then gone. The neighbours had begun gathering in the street, waiting for news, making a silent vigil. People bringing candles to light.

'Elderly people get upset when the news is on,' the nurse says.

Mum seems to be listening, but you can never know.

'They get so anxious and worried,' the nurse aide says. 'I don't know why they have the news channel on so much in the home. It puts ideas into their heads.'

Mum is quiet in the car; I'm pleased she doesn't mention the little girl any more. All I want, I say in my mind over and over, is to know why she let that bastard do what he did to me. Why didn't she take my side? I take a few turns around the town and drive her back to the home.

I'm at the petrol station the next day, filling the car up before my return journey, when someone from the home calls to ask if Mum is with me.

'No,' I say. 'I was about to call in and see her before we head back to Auckland.'

'Oh,' the woman says. 'She may be in the grounds but we can't find her.'

'Have you called the police?' I say.

She says the manager will call them, right now. They had just wanted to be sure she wasn't with me. A false alarm. 'Something might have unsettled her,' she adds. She means my visit. I don't get down here as much as I'd like. It's a long journey and you can't take too many days off work now there's this recession.

I hear another voice. She relays the message: 'Do you think she might have walked back to her old home?'

'It's quite a distance,' I say. 'Could she walk that far?'

'When they do take off like this, it can be surprising how far they can go,' the woman says. 'Almost like they're on the run…'

Like an escaped prisoner, I think.

The woman seems to realise what she's saying and instead pretends to cough. 'Would she even remember how to get there?'

'Well…' She's searching for something to say. 'Some of our residents do try to go back to their former homes. But it's more likely to happen when they've just moved in here and they're still unsettled.'

'I'll check.' Usually, I make a point of avoiding going that way. I phone Axel and tell him to get out of bed. I'll pick him up to help search.

First, I stop by the old house. It hasn't changed much. The new owners repainted the ugly maroon-coloured fence. They've got rid of the huge macrocarpa at the front. Its big powerful trunk, widely slashed, has been left in the ground. No one answers the doorbell, so I head around the back, along the concrete path. This is where I had to stand in the rain for an hour one night, in my thin pink nightdress; all because I hadn't turned the light off when Ivan called 'lights out'. Mum came to the window, twice, an unreadable expression on her face. It was the same expression she had when he thrashed some sense into me with a belt.

When I was allowed inside and he'd gone off to bed, she wrapped a blanket around me.

'Mum, he's a bastard, can't you see that?'

She sighed. Hard. Exasperated. 'You know what he expects.' Her face closed in on her. 'You shouldn't keep defying him.'

I didn't let myself cry this time. Just resolved I'd leave home as soon as I could. Turn my back on them for good. And the next time he thrashed me, I didn't look to Mum for anything.

The people who own the house now have demolished the old lean-to that was once our kitchen, the ground now cleared and bricked, replaced with a courtyard.

I return to my car and sit there shivering. Of course, in time I had returned to visit. You can't just shut your mother out of your life. But I'd given up trying to speak to her about it, never asked her why did she stay with him? My fingers shake as I turn the ignition key. The news is on; a senior police officer is finishing making an announcement at a press conference. It sounds like he's crying. I realise it must be the little girl who is missing he's talking about and I start to pay attention but it's too late, the segment is over.

My phone rings. 'Any sign?'

'No.'

'Is there anywhere else she might go?'

The school? But there's been no sign of her, a teacher taking PE in the playground tells me.

I don't tell Axel, my mother's missing till he gets in the car. He's about to tell me something, something he's seen on the Internet, but I head him off. I don't care. I don't want a conversation, not now, not while I am trying to think of any place Mum could be. I need to focus, I tell him. He can obviously hear how panicked I am about

Mum because he doesn't get shitty at me. Then I do think of some place she might be and I drive there as fast as I can.

I stop the car outside the park, on the harbour's edge. And there she is, sitting on a seat, near the swings. She's watching a man on a big ride-on lawn mower, making soft swathes in the green lawn. I run towards her. She doesn't seem surprised to see me.

'Mum,' I say, grabbing her by the elbow, feeling its tiny span. 'You had me scared to death. What were you thinking?'

Axel has followed me. 'Stop it,' he says. 'You're shouting at her.'

I feel my hand go slack on Mum, let her body slump back against the seat.

'The little girl,' she says.

'For God's sake, Mum,' I begin, but Axel cuts me off.

'Chill,' he says. I see that he is watching us both, an almost anxious expression on his face.

I shut up. Partly because he has told me to, but partly because from somewhere back in my memory, I am remembering a little girl. *The* little girl? The sea was grey that day, with white caps, and there were a few boats moored in the harbour, bobbing about in the tide. It was a cold, frosty morning. No one around. I wasn't at school for some reason. We stopped at the park for Raymond to have a swing.

She was sitting on one of the low swings. Just sitting, not swinging.

'This is where the little girl was,' I say now to my mother.

'Yes.'

The girl was wearing a pink top and bottom. Outside on a cold wintry day in the park in her PJs. They had a rabbit on the top part.

I remember that my mother went over to her and asked her if she was lost. The little girl put her thumb in her mouth. Mum told me to take my jacket off and put it around her.

Now Mum sits here, watching the man on the motor mower.

'You said we were going to wait there until her mum came looking.'

'Yes.'

We waited a long time. Then Mum said to me that we'd take her to the police station. It was so cold. It seemed ages after she said this, and we were still waiting at the park, when a woman came. She was a large woman — fat is what I remember — and was pushing a big white pram with a baby in it. She came up and started yelling at the girl for something.

Mum stood even closer to the little girl. She said that we had waited with the little girl because she was on her own; it could be dangerous in the park. The woman got all blustery. She said she'd told the girl to wait at the other end of the park for a few minutes while she went to the shop for a bottle of milk. 'She dawdles so much it was quicker to race over and get it by myself. It was only a few minutes, for God's sake.' That's what the woman said. 'Not that it's anything to do with you,' she said. She lurched towards Mum and I was scared.

The thing I remember the most was that Mum didn't take fright when the woman was so ugly and loud and had begun ranting. She didn't back away.

And somehow, though even now I don't know how it happened, the woman started just talking. She talked and talked and she went on and on and I gave up listening in because I had a feeling that whatever Mum had done, it had calmed her down.

Now I say to Mum. 'It was you who found the little girl,' I say.

I turn to Axel who is standing there quietly. I can see he is awkward, doesn't know what to do. 'I remember hearing Mum tell someone at the church about the woman,' I say. 'She'd said the woman's husband had left her. There was no money coming in and it was hard.'

Mum has lost interest. I can see the dullness come over her face. She has gone somewhere else. But I know that for a long time after, Mum used to drop off boxes of vegetables from our garden to a house near the park. It had a veranda roof that was about to collapse.

For the first time — it embarrasses me to acknowledge this, for the first time probably ever — it hits me. 'It *was* hard, wasn't it,

23

Mum?' I ask slowly. It feels strange that despite being a grown woman, a single mother myself, this is the first time the thought has occurred to me. 'If you didn't have a husband, there was no money. No benefits. You'd be just on your own.'

'Yes,' Mum says. She seems to shrug. Then she peers at me in a way that makes me think she is trying to ask have I any more questions?

None, I think. Because now I see there is no point. It's like that expression she was so fond of, 'If you can't change it, don't complain.' Get yourself up and get going. That was Mum's way of dealing with life.

'Let's go, Mum,' I say, and I help her up from the seat. Her feet drag as she walks and I can see all the puff has gone out of her. It has been a major journey for her, re-tracing her steps to the park.

Axel waits till we get back to the car before he says anything. 'Hey,' he says diffidently enough, but there's something in his tone. 'I looked up UFO sightings. There were some here — back in the 60s. And the 50s, too. A lot of people saw them.'

'You're kidding me,' I say.

'Nah,' he says. 'There's been a Government report. About a month ago, listing all the sightings. Heaps.'

'She *did* see a UFO.' I'm saying the words to myself really. My voice sounds like it's not me. Like I am a little girl again.

'I sure did.' Mum has spoken an entire sentence. Her voice no longer sounds deep and faraway. She looks at me and nods as if finally, something between us has been settled.

The Ring – Linda Bennett

Mirry is sweating. Her salmon-pink dress encloses her like plastic wrapped round a chunk of fish and the straps of her high-heeled sandals are buried in the flesh that hides her ankles. She shifts her weight from one foot to the other, leaning on the handle of the wheelchair. But she is not careful enough. Gus Chaplin turns faded blue eyes towards her, irritation wrinkling his lips.

'Sit, Mirry.'

She shakes her head. She will not leave her spot to lumber three feet to the pew behind them. It is bad enough that she is trapped up front for the ceremony. Her hope is that if she remains still, she will be blessed with invisibility.

'I'm fine,' she says, pitching her voice sharp and low. Let the old boy hear it and shut up.

But he won't let go. 'Don't be stupid, girl. Vi will probably be late. You should sit down, take a load off.'

Gus Chaplin has many good qualities, but tactfulness is not one of them. This she knows, so she ignores his words and takes refuge behind the mask she has worn for the past three years: dedicated caregiver, hardworking nurse's aide. Her elderly charges don't mind what she looks like; in fact, she sometimes thinks they don't really see her at all.

'Don't worry, Gus. She'll be here soon enough.'

'It's not her I'm worried about.' Gus tugs at his bowtie for the third time in ten minutes. 'It's you. You're red as a beet, girl. Can't have my wedding ruined by you keeling over at the altar.' He works his mouth for a moment, as if he's considering summoning an usher to have her removed. 'It's too damn hot in here. We should have waited for autumn.'

'I'll be fine.' She stares ahead, gaze skimming over the daisies and roses that litter the front of the chapel. Above them, framed within a stained-glass window, Jesus gazes down at her, his smile fixed, his halo gleaming in the afternoon light. She looks away. She doesn't want the eyes of this translucent God upon her, judging her for what she has become.

The flowers shimmer and dance in the heat. The straps of Mirry's bra are cutting into her shoulders and she can feel beads of sweat forming on her upper lip. Dear God, she prays, have mercy on me and get that woman down the aisle quick. As if in answer to her prayer, Mendelssohn's wedding march booms out with a ferocity that startles her. Violet Poole has arrived at the back of the chapel on the arm of her grandson, Michael. She's a roly-poly blob of a woman, with a pale face and a large mole on the side of her nose. As they start down the aisle, Mirry gets her first proper look at the lanky grandson whose baby pictures dot the bookshelf in Violet's room. He is, Violet has told her with pride, training to be a minister. Mirry expects a pallid pastoral type in glasses and a shabby suit.

But this boy is no pale-skinned, mealy-mouthed cleric. Michael Poole is a self-assured young man whose dark gray suit makes him look both elegant and tough as steel. His hair has been tamed with water and there are deep shadows beneath his eyes. As his gaze sweeps across the chapel, Mirry flushes. He's the kind of man who always unsettles her, makes her wish she could disappear into the carpet.

She will not look at Violet, dare not look at Michael. So she turns to Gus, who will need her help to stand as he waits for his bride to totter down the aisle. She reaches out a hand, but Gus is rising from his chair faster than a jack rabbit. She stares at him, but it is not his unexpected agility that surprises her.

It is the look on his face that takes her breath away.

With hands laced across his chest as if he is trying to still his heart, Gus Chaplin gazes up the aisle at Violet Poole. He is glowing, his eyes damp. As Violet moves down the aisle, Mirry sees Gus's lips quiver, watches him bite down hard to keep the emotions in check.

But tears and smiles make a mess of his face and he snorts, fumbling in his pocket for a dark-blue handkerchief.

Mirry stares at her feet — ten stubby toes tipped with red and squashed into a pair of fancy sandals — and feels despair sinking like stone to the empty pit of her stomach. She has lost count of the number of times she has begged God to take away her fat, to make her beautiful — to make her lovable.

Michael Poole and his grandmother arrive next to Gus and Mirry. The chapel is filled with rustles and coughs as the elderly guests release walkers and canes and settle back into the pews. Gus and Violet join hands, their fingers entwined like teenagers, Violet smiles at Gus and the minister is a beaming blur of black and white in front of them. From the window above, Jesus watches them with his unblinking eyes.

'...gathered together in the Presence of God...' The minister's voice rebounds off the walls and after a brief inner wrestle, Mirry sneaks a look at Michael. His grandmother still clings to his arm, and he covers her hand, stroking her fingers with his own. As if he feels her gaze on him, Michael looks up and catches Mirry peeking at him. Heat rushes up her neck into her face, and she jerks her eyes away. As she does so, he smiles at her, but it's a meaningless all-purpose kind of smile. Hot with humiliation, Mirry longs to disappear, but she is glued to the floor by her bulk and her role in this ceremony. She tries to concentrate on what the minister is saying.

'...to have and to hold ... in sickness and in health ... to love and to cherish, till death us do part...'

As the service unfolds and the sun slants lower through the stained-glass window, Mirry feels dizzy and wonders if she is going to faint. But then Gus turns towards her and extends his hand. She reaches into her purse, steps forward and places the ring on his outstretched palm.

The old man smiles and his hand trembles. The ring glitters in the sunlight, a seal of love given and received. Mirry is relieved. Her part is done. She steps back towards the pew.

'Oh my — Mirry…'

Gus's hand is empty, his mouth agape. Mirry turns her head, sees the band of gold skipping across the cold floor towards the heavy, ornately-carved altar table.

Mirry looks up. Violet now has both hands welded to Michael's arm. Gus is groping for his wheelchair, confusion creasing his face. The minister clutches his Bible to his breast like a shield.

Nobody moves. Mirry feels a nauseating disbelief as she realizes she's the one who'll have to retrieve the ring. She sets her purse down on the pew, knowing by the burn in her face that everyone is watching her.

As she faces the walk to the table, a tide of anger catches her unawares. She wants to grab Gus round his scrawny neck and curse him for his stupidity and clumsiness. She glances at Violet, sees her mouth hanging open like a codfish, and thinks she'd like to strangle her, too. What right has she to such happiness, at her age?

Mirry storms forward, sandals clacking on the tiles, pink dress rustling round her legs. She reaches the table and peers behind it, but the ring has rolled deep in and she cannot see it. Humiliation swamps her as she gets down on her knees. She swipes her hand beneath the table, praying for the touch of cool metal beneath her fingers. But there is nothing.

She will have to go lower to find the ring. Immediately she knows that if she does, the bridal party will be treated to the sight of her rear end swaying to and fro as she gropes beneath the table. And her rear end, swathed in yards of salmon pink chiffon, is not a pretty sight. Shame and rage sweep through her and she wants to run, screaming, from the chapel. But she is trapped by her fat, her faults and her failings.

The silence is broken by tiny rustlings and muffled coughs. People are becoming restless. What does she have to lose, that she hasn't already lost? She goes down flat on the floor, prostrate in front of the altar table. The smell of polish is in her nose and the floor is cool beneath her chin.

28

She wriggles forward and sweeps her arm under the table. Her fingers brush against something smooth and cold and she pulls her arm out, anxious to be up and moving again.

In her hand is a tiny glass, stained with the dregs of communion wine.

She wants to scream. She wants to let rip with a string of curses that will sear elderly ears and force the clerics to adjust their plastic collars. Instead, hot pricking tears threaten to spill from her eyes. She blinks and goes back to trying to find the ring with her fingers. Then, high above her on the wall she sees another Jesus. But this Jesus wears neither halo nor translucent smile. This Jesus is trapped, nailed to a rough-hewn cross, his face is contorted with agony. Sweat drips from his brow and through her tears, it seems as if he is struggling to free himself. I know how you feel, she tells him, as her fingers quest to and fro. Life's a bitch and then you die.

Mirry's fingers close upon a circle of cold metal. She pulls her arm free from beneath the table, sits up and wipes her eyes with the back of her hand.

'Well done.' Now, when it's all over, Michael Poole squats at her side and offers her his hand. His eyes are dark brown, and crease up at the corners as he smiles at her. 'Let me help you.'

He slides an arm around her and lifts her to her feet as if she weighs no more than a feather. He retrieves the little glass from the floor and sets it on the table. She hears the squeak of his shoes, catches the scent of mint on his breath as he takes the ring from her. Minutes later, Gus and Vi are pronounced man and wife and the wedding ceremony is over.

Mirry blows her nose and wonders what she's supposed to do next. She sees Michael enfolding his grandmother in a hug while the minister shakes Gus's hand. Guests move down the aisle, smiles of congratulation on their lips. In a flurry of black and white, the minister turns and sweeps over to her.

'Well done, Mirry dear — thank you so much.'

He bustles away and Mirry sees Gus beckoning her over. 'What a clumsy old man you must think me, Mirry. I'm so sorry.'

'It's OK.' Mirry wrinkles her nose at the camphorated scent of his moth-balled suit. 'It's nothing.'

He takes her hand and pats it, like a dog. 'We're having a party now. Come, have a glass of champagne.'

As she turns to wheel Gus up the aisle, Mirry sees a swathe of coloured light falling across the floor in front of them and she looks up. From the window high above them, his halo glowing in the late afternoon light, the stained-glass Jesus smiles down on her. Mirry stares back. Then she straightens up her shoulders and turns her back to the window.

'Sweet as, Gus,' she says, nodding, as they set off down the aisle behind Violet and Michael. 'Party time it is.'

In Bath, in Autumn – Gay Buckingham

A week in Bath in autumn: orange cheddar and local scrumpie; the creamy, curving Royal Crescent and Jane Austen memorabilia.

He told me it was his meteorological symposium at the university: he meant it was time for me to move on from my grief-stricken paralysis.

It was kindly meant; he was willing me to jump on an escalator which would move me along from Present to Before. As if Before was a place I could go. There was, too, desperation in his invitation — could he survive with this wife whose smile had become a grimace and whose silences could last for days because she had forgotten how to speak.

I would try. For his sake I would go to Before if I could.

We are accommodated in a voluptuous terrace house, brochure description: 'finest Georgian chic'. It is amongst a street of classical John Wood the Younger limestone dwellings, which glow mellow golden in the late summer warmth.

The registrar has arranged for photos in full academic regalia and then we circulate, clutching stemmed glasses. The colours and formality seem exaggerated, but we dutifully mingle, and are appropriately condescended to.

— so, as in Europe, Antipodean universities garb their graduands in gowns, hoods and caps. How quaint —

I turn away.

— the pineapple motif, grafted onto that of the acorn — goodness, what a spontaneously apt metaphor —

I push past.

— the radiating cumulus ascends —

— the culmination of such excess is inordinately —

Now I'm shoving.

— even drama students at the Barbican —

— post-modernists appreciate —

Through one door. Through closed fire doors. Leaning my face against the cool glass. Slow the heart. Breathe. Breathe again. Quiet. Think snow on mountains. Stillness and whiteness. Slow glaciers and the Southern Alps. And thwacking hospital doors, pristine coverlets smoothed on beds, a cloth covering her shape and drooping over the edge of the trolley.

He is kind to me: understanding.

— First try. Hard, but you've done it. Next time will be easier.

His recovery prescription is easy to adhere to. While he attends the opening forum I will go on a guided walk. The guide is of Indian extraction and it seems right and proper that, as the Romans colonised the Britons, and the British colonised India, Jhumpa could show us the spring where Celts worshipped Sulis.

— Now, if you look over and across at those buildings, she says, you will see they removed windows because citizens were taxed on the number of windows they had.

I gaze at them. Sightless.

— Bath was known for the haunts and habits of Beau Brummell, foremost in a society of fops, fools and fashion, she adds, then points to the conical extrusions on top of fences, along ledges and under eaves.

— These can be interpreted as acorns, pinecones or pineapples

So nothing is certain.

We finish with a walk over shop-littered Poulteney Bridge, and meekly return to our starting point at the Pump House. I buy a genuine Roman coin, and then a Sally Lunn bun to have with my cup of tea. Is it my throat or the bun which is so dry? I persevere and it doesn't choke me.

I don't want to go back to my finest Georgian flat screen television, so retreat to the canal, pausing to crumple down on the grass beside the lock. Like me it is sluggish in the afternoon ease and I doze, rousing myself to observe the white geese, creamy white, reminding me of that deceptive pallor. There are five of them and they have flown in from the south, landed on the water and are now drifting. I believe there is a river further down, but here the canal broadens and I turn my gaze from the geese to a messy floating pile of rubbish, plastic bottles and sticks. It is the nest of a late-rearing grebe and that makes me think of down, and downy heads, but I must banish these thoughts.

It's been stressed that any activity is good activity, and some photos would be evidence I have been trying to alleviate my numbness so I take up my camera and line up these benign pale birds — but the battery is flat. Here, in time immemorial, I cannot cement even one moment.

Our hotel boasts 'interconnectivity' in every room, but that doesn't help me to get to Before and I don't try. I nap, and then am determinedly alert at dinner. Indeed you might say that I am gay. So gay I reiterate people's names in conversation to show I've been paying attention at introductions and I continue to pay attention, turning my head this way and that to follow conversations round the table and proffer contributions — but then find myself laughing immoderately before a punch line. I try to deflect the storyteller's disconcerted stare.

— The story reminds me of a joke I have heard before, I say to him — and the attentive table.

— But I must confess that I cannot retell it — or not in a way that would do it justice.

I am over compensating. He — they — continue to gaze at me. Perhaps they think there is no such story — that I am drunk — or, more charitably, that I suffer from some sort of nervous disposition.

My husband knows better. Under the table he holds my trembling fingers in his hand, running his thumb over the pulse of my wrist. He rescues me by asking the woman on my left about the Museum of Costume and soon the group is talking about the Bath Museum of Eastern Art, and then the American Museum. He has extricated me from my gauche attempts at normality, but it reinforces for me that I will not attend the following day's plenary session when he will give his address. I would like to go to listen — to watch, support, bear witness, whatever — but I know his attention must not be deflected into protecting me, and that is fairer that I do not attend. I don't tell him my decision.

And so next day I go to the American Museum. The bus route takes in the university and one student turns and addresses the other passengers before she disembarks: she speaks of carbon footprints and bio-diesel. But it is a terse statement and I do not catch her intention, whether she is commending or reproving. The other students ignore her and continue to pass cryptic phrases between themselves, without context and meriting no response, so that I am in an existential vacuum as the hydraulic door whooshes open to set me down on the edge of a wooded ridge, beside a sign announcing the entrance drive to the American Museum.

It's of fairly modest aspect — or it is compared to what I have already seen — and there is no dearth of information at the entrance, but I ignore the brochures and souvenirs. I am here to fill in the hours till lunchtime. Then there will be three more days of this conference; I can't think that far.

Now the smell of gingerbread pervades everything. It is sweet and warm and I enter a room to find a woman with a fancy mob-cap and long grey skirt beside a stove which has blue and white delft tiles.

— Martha Washington's very own recipe, she says. Have a piece.

It will choke me but it seems churlish to refuse.

— This is what her kitchen at Mt Vernon would have been like. This is the sort of food she would have had served. Of course she had slaves, we don't think of her like that, do we? But she did.

I eat the crumbly cake and don't gag as she tells me in her soft accent there are more rooms to see.

— The American experience, she explains. This is the only museum of Americana outside of the United States.

I am in Bath and am to experience a kaleidoscope of period homes of the citizens of the land of the free.

The Frontier room has an iron stove and a coonskin cap thrown on a wooden stool. Sparse Shaker simplicity is a relief after a nineteenth century parlour with antimacassars and ferns on tall stands. Then I come to the quilts.

They hang on walls and display-stands and are very old, precisely stitched bedcovers of browns and rusty reds. They are the colour of dried blood. Each represents great patience and an enormous amount of some forgotten woman's time, a woman who would have seamed and pieced despite lost husbands, sons dying in blood and agony, brothers gone forever into an unknown wilderness. These quilts may have comforted their daughters in fever, wrapped those who would die in childbirth, were constructed and gifted in celebration of betrothal and marriage. They were sewn despite fires and violence, with or without the balm of religion. These are the drear colours of birth, menstruation, injury and death.

I know what dried blood looks like and what death looks like. I know about the hardships of generations of women and don't need to immerse myself in this, yet I can't leave the room of quilts. A sign requests visitors not to touch but my hand is drawn to one close-by. I dare not touch it. The label says that particular pattern is called 'sunburst' and it's dated circa 1790. Tiny running stitches outline a series of concentric circles around the edges and then inside that they follow the edges of each patch, and the patterns within them, as they channel into the centred star.

It is a mandala of life's wholeness.

I stay in the quiet room for a very long time. It is still. I am still. Stillness. I breathe. And again. Faded fabric; desiccated russet dyes; shriven stuff. Yet this is what our lives are made of.

Eventually I leave and go back to Cheap St, to wait for the audience to spill out of the auditorium. As he comes towards me I note there is a buoyancy in the way people greet him, defer, but he takes my arm to lead me away from them. Somehow we have entered the abbey, where a group of young men are singing a cappella, something that sounds like Bach.

— I looked for you, he says.

I want to explain.

— While I spoke my eyes scanned the front seats, the row behind, but you weren't there. And I kept looking in the seats further back, in the gallery and on the steps, everywhere. But you weren't there.

I can't speak. I look at him.

Around us pure sound soars up to the great fan vaulted ceiling and rebounds on stone and wood. Young voices resound into beauty, become a symphony of passion, witnesses to what the soul can achieve.

— Not anywhere. And when they clapped, when they said those things, I wanted you on the podium beside me. I cannot change the past —

His voice breaks, and he looks at me as if he were searching for me still.

— And I cannot face this future.

And I take his arms and I put them around me and I can taste the salt of his tears as they trickle into my mouth, which, though open, still can't speak. I link his fingers in mine and they knot tightly as we crush our hands, our faces, our bodies.

— The tiny body that came out of ours, creamy and waxy, has left us, he says.

— But as her birth was her gift of love, so can her death be our gift of love.

I want to tell him the quilts have taught me that, but we are overpowered by the young men's voices, which increase in volume, circling and weaving into a yet greater crescendo. It is a welling of aching, overpowering beauty, of soaring and swamping purity. We weep, for her little mangled body and those crumpled limbs, and for each other, a breaking surge of grief which rises, soars, and peaks with the music, then peels off, sheaf after sheaf, stripping away every layer till there is only love, for each other, and the child, and the love she left us.

We can't have Before. We have now.

You Look Beautiful When You Smile – Celia Coyne

Ever since Happiness heard your name, he has been running through the streets trying to find you. He saw you on a sunny morning, striding down Mount Pleasant, slowing only to avoid the spongy tarmac where a burst pipe was sending water to the surface. You were moving fast, your head held high, taking in the view over Christchurch to the mountains beyond. The air was clear with the occasional waft of sweet lemon from the autumn-flowering shrubs. Happiness almost caught up with you, but you gave him the slip at the bottom of the hill, stepping neatly over the bricks where the path had unzipped. He was left standing at the side of the road, waiting for a gap in the traffic.

The roadworks on the bridge were causing chaos and no one was giving way, and when he finally managed to get across the road, you were almost at the bus-stop. You frowned as you walked past the vast empty space that used to be the Countdown supermarket. It was full of light, its remaining concrete pillars making a frame for the sky, but you were looking at the rubble. You looked so sad as you got on the bus to Sumner that you made Happiness sigh. He kept his distance.

But Happiness is the eternal optimist, so he followed you to Sumner that day, taking the next bus and enjoying the view out over the ocean. Listless lenticular clouds were moving slowly along the horizon. Their elongated forms were tinged with shades of green and blue, reflecting off the lagoon. When he got to the town, you had bought yourself an iced coffee and were drinking it as you walked along the seafront. But then you had to make a detour round the tall protective fencing near Cave Rock and he lost sight of you again. The next thing he knew you were taking a short cut past one of those large, rusty shipping containers that line the road beside the cliffs.

When he looked, all he could see back there were damp shadows and the chance of a rock fall. He didn't feel comfortable at all. So he called it a day.

The next time he saw you, you were window-shopping in Cashel Street. The temporary shops in converted containers looked trendy and bright. They sparkled in the sunlight, offering up their shelves of colourful, if overpriced, trinkets. There were a lot of people around and Happiness had to thread his way through a gaggle of tourists who were being very slow and photographing everything. He was carrying a big bunch of flowers (yellow roses, your favourite), so couldn't have been more conspicuous, yet you were oblivious. But the tourists were delighted with him and insisted on a group photo, smiling and pleading amicably. He obliged and by the time he'd finished you had moved off and were well on your way to the park.

Now Happiness is no quitter. He broke into a run, catching you at the entrance gate. He was quite out of puff when he handed you the flowers, but still managed a winning smile.

That was when you said, after reading the note attached: 'You must be mistaken, they can't be for me. Who would give me flowers? It's not my birthday or anything.' And you wouldn't take them. Refused point blank. You had a look in your eye that said you thought he was a nutcase, could be dangerous, and so he backed off. He gave the flowers to a little old lady who was sitting on a bench feeding sparrows. It made her day.

'Yellow is for friendship,' she said.

Happiness was perplexed. You were a tough nut to crack. But he wouldn't give up; it was his job, after all. He had heard your name, knew you by heart, and he had faith that he would find you again. He remained vigilant and ready. A few days later he spotted you at the Book Exchange Fridge that stands on the concrete foundations of what was once a house. He could see you standing in the mellow autumn light, your face serene. After all this chasing, he did not want to frighten you off, so he held back for a moment. You were pulling out books from the converted fridge, leafing through them and putting them back. But before he could approach, there came a roar as a 4.9 aftershock rumbled through. He watched the pavement hump up and down in one smooth movement as the tremor passed by. Amazing! he thought, but in that moment of distraction he lost you. When he looked up, you were no longer there.

It was clear that Happiness would have to try something different. He became crafty. He would use your friends to get to you. It was an old trick that had worked before. He whispered to Suzie to put a note on Facebook — 'Join me at the Dance-o-mat.'

The Dance-o-mat was one of Happiness's favourite places in Christchurch. It was situated in the cleared ground of a clothes store. Someone had put down a dance floor and converted a commercial washing machine so that people could put a gold coin in the slot and play music through loud speakers. Happiness liked the crowds that turned up there; and since he had broad tastes in music he could happily, excuse the pun, spend hours there. This time he didn't follow you; he waited for you to arrive. And you did, with a group of your friends.

You look beautiful, he thought, when you smile. In his experience, most people do.

He watched as you put your money in the slot, hooked up your iPod and started clowning about to the music. More people turned up, some of them in fancy dress and Happiness felt right at home. After a while he managed to talk to you, sharing a joke. You said you had a funny feeling that you'd met him before.

And you danced with him for ages.

(First line courtesy of the Iranian poet Hafiz c1320.)

What Anton Learns in the Queue – Janis Freegard

At eleven minutes past three, Anton joins the queue. He's wearing his new blue shirt and the old straw boater his mum gave him years ago. Anton's height is approximately 1.86 metres, his age twenty-nine. The queue is for one of two portable toilets, which the organisers of 'Music in the Park' have deemed sufficient to cater for the needs of an estimated 800 people. The estimate is Anton's own and includes, somewhere, his girlfriend, Shell, who has wandered off to find coffee. He enjoys making educated guesses of this kind — the size of crowds, the expected duration of a wait in line. He has attached himself to the queue at this point, not because he needs the toilet now, but because after the three beers he has consumed this afternoon, he expects to need it in half an hour's time. Which is approximately how long it is likely to take before he gets to the front of the line.

Anton plays tenor sax in a jazz band called Jazz Jivin. Anton did not choose the name; he thinks it's a stupid name. But he likes the music they play and he likes being in a band. They have been playing together for over a year now, and they're getting quite good. In Anton's opinion, they could be even better if his fellow band members would consent to practising four times a week instead of twice, but he has been unable to persuade them to do so. They will, however, be playing later this afternoon at 'Music in the Park'. Anton thinks he had probably better not have any more beer, in case it affects his ability to remember his notes.

The band on now is playing a blend of funk and reggae. This is the ideal sort of music for Anton's band to follow. The crowd will be nicely chilled. In front of the stage, a young Pākehā woman in tie-dyed trousers and a pink op-shop slip is twirling some kind of long poi in time to the beat. A man with blonde dreads juggles oranges. A

41

slim, shirtless Māori guy with a goatee is swaying to the rhythm, his head lifted skywards, eyes closed.

Third in front of him in the toilet queue is a perfect woman. Which is to say, a woman who conforms to Anton's ideas of physical perfection. Her face is turned towards the stage and Anton has a good view of that face in profile. Her soft pink lipstick has been immaculately applied. Her lips look like peony petals. She's wearing form-fitting designer clothes and high-heeled boots. Everyone else there is barefoot or sandaled. Classy, is the word that springs to Anton's mind. She's likely to get to the toilets six and a half minutes before Anton does, allowing for the fact that women always take longer. Anton wonders how long she spends putting on make-up and choosing what to wear each day. He estimates a good half-hour for the make-up and perhaps another twenty minutes for dressing, depending on the perfect woman's level of decisiveness.

Anton's girlfriend, Shell, rarely wears lipstick and puts on whatever is closest to hand when she gets up (invariably late) in the morning. It takes Shell an average of four-and-a-half minutes to get ready. Anton wishes she would wear high-heeled boots sometimes. He's been pointing them out when they walk past shoe stores, but Shell isn't taking the hint.

Anton and Shell have been going out for almost a year now and Anton is seriously considering asking her to move in with him, or rather for them to find a place together. He's never lived with anyone, never wanted to, but he's nearly thirty now and it seems like the right time. But he wishes Shell would just take a bit more interest in her appearance. Maybe he could buy her some lipstick.

There are children running about, clambering up trees and dancing in front of the stage. Little wild children with tanned bodies and noses coated in sun-block. A small boy of about two walks up to Anton on slightly unsteady feet and stares intently at Anton's straw hat. Anton wonders where the child's parents are. The small boy giggles and claps his hands. A pregnant woman appears from nowhere and scoops up the laughing boy, turning him upside down

42

so his hair almost touches the grass. The boy squeals delightedly. It occurs to Anton that a large part of childhood is taken up with trying to escape your parents and then being glad when they find you and take you back. He touches his hat and an image of his own mother flashes into his mind. Did she ever turn him upside down like that? He feels sad that he can't remember.

A shadow creeps along the line by the portable toilets. Anton looks up to see clouds gathering. Typical. It's going to rain on their gig. Everyone will leave. Jazz Jivin doesn't get the chance to play to a crowd this size very often. Anton's day will be ruined.

The queue variously spreads and branches. Pockets of friends and acquaintances chat as they wait; some move to the music. Anton is starting to feel the pressure on his bladder. He estimates another fifteen minutes to the head of the line. He was sensible to start queuing when he did. One of his fellow Jazz Jivers simply wandered off towards some bushes and recommended that Anton do the same. Anton's too shy, though. He can't even use a urinal if there's another man there. He just dries up.

Directly behind him, a woman with Down's syndrome attaches herself to the queue. She's wearing a yellow sundress and carrying a green vinyl handbag that reminds him of a lollipop. She looks about twenty, but it's hard to tell. Anton tries not to look at her. He's never known any people like that. It seems sad.

He feels a tap on his shoulder and turns around. 'What's your name?' she asks with a radiant smile. Anton glances about, hoping there's a relative or care-giver somewhere. But she seems to be alone.

'Anton,' he answers, a little too loudly perhaps. He wonders if anyone's looking.

'Oh what a lovely name!' the young woman exclaims. 'Anton. Oh, that's beautiful.'

Anton wishes she'd just queue in silence, like everyone else. He feels obliged to reciprocate. 'And what's your name?'

'Bernadette.'

'That's a nice name too.' People are looking at them. He hopes no one thinks he knows her.

'Thank you, Anton. Thank you.' Bernadette beams.

Anton realises he will be stuck with her behind him for the next twelve minutes or so. He considers leaving the queue altogether, but realises he can't spare the time. His band is going on at four. They need twenty minutes to set up; it would be cutting it too fine.

'Have you got a girlfriend, Anton?'

Oh Jesus, surely she's not flirting with him? 'Yes, I have got a girlfriend. Her name's Shell.'

'Do you love her, Anton?'

What a question! Bernadette is staring at him intently, waiting for his answer as though it's the most important question in the world. Maybe it is.

He thinks about the day he met Shell, at a flatmate's birthday dinner. How struck he'd been by her *alive*-ness, how she was full of energy and ideas. She was talking about her travels in Thailand and her plans to visit India, to work in an orphanage there that a New Zealand woman had helped set up. She waved her hands as she talked and Anton remembers thinking that even her hair looked lively. Coiled springs, eager to escape the hair band she was wearing. He wonders for a moment what it would be like not to have Shell in his life and it's like being punched in the chest. 'Yes,' he tells Bernadette. 'Yes, I suppose I do love her.'

Bernadette is moving her body in time to the reggae beat. He's surprised at how well she can dance. 'This is such a good song,' she says. 'Anton, isn't this a good song?'

'Yeah, great song,' Anton replies. Bernadette's smile is catching.

'Do you want to dance, Anton?'

Oh shit. The queue is visible to the whole eight hundred strong crowd. What will people think?

'Come on Anton!' She looks so happy. In fact, she looks like the happiest person Anton has ever seen. What's she got to be so cheerful about? he wonders. Why aren't I as happy as that? Two young women from the queue start dancing with her.

The sky rumbles like a growling Alsatian. The clouds that had threatened, break. Anton looks into the crowd for Shell's face, but can't locate her. Next to him, Bernadette raises her arms to the sky and says cheerfully, 'Oh look, Anton, it's raining!'

Suddenly, Anton's back to childhood. That day it pelted down. Driving home from the hospital. Mum trying to smile, saying, the doctor estimates six months. Six months. He remembers working it out: 26 weeks, 182 days. And then back home, Dad outside in the rain, mowing the same patch of lawn over and over. In the end, the doctor's estimate turned out to be 47 days too generous.

As the crowd scatters for shelter under the few awnings and trees, Anton struggles to see the rain through Bernadette's eyes. She's opening her mouth to catch raindrops, still dancing. He recognises the same delight he caught on the face of the little boy being scooped up by his mother earlier. We must be born with it, thinks Anton, born with a love for life. Then somewhere along the line, it gets battered out of us. Bernadette is turning around in circles, arms outstretched. Anton estimates she's rotated herself twenty times already — a total of seven thousand two hundred degrees. How can rotating yourself in the rain put so much joy on a person's face?

It strikes him that he needn't feel sorry for her at all. To be honest, he's starting to envy her. There's always someone better off than yourself, he thinks. But it can surprise you to find out who it is. Anton lets his body bend a little to the music.

Bernadette falls over on to the wet grass from too much spinning and laughs. Anton looks to see if anyone's going to help her. No-one's coming. It'll have to be him. He reaches out a hand to pull her up. But instead of taking it, she looks at him thoughtfully, then rummages through her green vinyl bag. She pulls out a pair of cheap plastic sunglasses with yellow lenses and waves them at him. 'Put these on Anton,' she says. 'Everything looks different.'

'It's all right, thanks.' They look like they've come from the two dollar shop.

Bernadette looks up at him with her head to one side. 'Are you happy, Anton?'

He considers the question. It's raining buckets and his band might not get to play. He loves his girlfriend but she doesn't wear boots. A young woman with Down's syndrome wants him to wear a pair of sunglasses that are guaranteed to make him look stupid in front of a large crowd.

'When you put these on, everything goes sunny.'

Oh, to hell with it, thinks Anton. Why not? He slides Bernadette's sunglasses over his ears and his world turns yellow. Everything does look different. It's still wet, but now it doesn't seem to matter so much.

He thinks: what if I just decide: right, I'm having it back. The joie de vivre that's my birthright. What if I just choose to be happy? I've got a wonderful girlfriend; I play in a jazz band, like I've always wanted to. I live in one of the best cities in the world; and even though the weather's packed up, the whole park looks bright.

'Told you,' says Bernadette. She's back on her feet now, giggling and twirling. A few others from the queue have joined in. The woman with the long poi emerges from the sheltering trees and adds herself to the group. Even the perfect woman with the boots and the peony lipstick is turning in circles and smiling. The shirtless man with the goatee claps his hands and shouts, *yeah*!

Anton closes his eyes behind the yellow lenses and starts spinning his body in time to the beat, arms stretched out in the rain. It feels good. He inhales the scent of the wet grass and it takes him back again. A different scene. His grandparents' house at the beach. Granddad watering the vege garden, Grandma spreading grass clippings around the roses. Granddad coming up behind her and planting a big kiss on top of her sunhat, his eyes all crinkly with love.

Anton remembers what his mum said to him, near the end. Find someone who makes you happy.

'Anton, you're dancing! That's great, Anton,' says Bernadette.

And so he is. Because there are some things, like rain, that you just can't change. So you might as well dance your way through them.

Anton feels a grin forming. He opens his eyes in time to see Shell coming towards him, barefoot on the wet grass. He estimates she's just a hug away.

Game Face – Lilla Csorgo

I dreamt of you again last night. We were outside, lying on the ground, staring up at the night sky. We were no longer a couple but your legs bridged mine, close but not touching. There were thousands of stars but there was one area where they were clustered more densely than I had ever seen. Just as I pointed this out to you, a meteor shower started and the sky was filled with falling stars. And you asked me, 'What did you wish for?' and I responded, 'What I always wish for.'

Travis lurked around the corner from Cosmos, staring at his watch, reluctant to move.

He was late. Travis was always late and Andi was incapable of being anything but punctual even though she knew she would only be kept waiting. Thank God she had her phone, even if she didn't have any messages to check, emails to clear, and was too scared of the embarrassment of being caught playing Angry Birds. So she stared at the menu, knowing already what she would order — a coffee — the phone safely on the table by the menu's side.

She was grateful that Travis insisted on meeting during the day. Much better than after work when it would have caused talk. None of it good. She would have, however, preferred Starbucks, where the wait staff — baristas — spoke pseudo Italian behind high counters, cutting themselves off from the transaction. At Cosmos the waitresses wore retro pink polyester and frilly aprons. Snapping gum — it seemed to be part of the uniform — they came to you, giving Travis occasion to gawk, flirt, his whole body twisted towards them.

Travis resisted the urge not to enter. She was already there. Why did she always already have to be there? Why couldn't he too feel the luxury of having been put upon? He stopped halfway across the café. It was a big place. Travis liked that. Allowed more time for an entrance. He chatted with Cathy. He didn't remember her from last time but her name was helpfully written right there on her name tag, which he managed to read while pretending to check out her breasts. Which weren't bad even if he suspected the bra was padded. They almost always were. Still, they gave him hope. No not hope, the strength to cross the rest of the room and sit down at Andi's table. She always chose the same one, skulking in the corner.

Andi watched Travis cross the room. It's why she always chose the table at the back, so that she wouldn't miss one moment of his performance. It's what he wanted. An audience. And she was willing to provide it. It gave her strength to watch him perform. The villain of the piece so that she could be the ingénue. The feisty ingénue.

'How about those Leafs?' he asked. This is what he always asked. Except in summer when he asked, 'How about those Jays?' He was being ironic. It was their little joke, apart from neither of them finding it funny.

They had been forced upon each other. The firm in its wisdom thought that they should be 'buddies'. This was the term they actually used. Even in written correspondence. Without the quotation marks, although one sensed that they were still there. The firm itself not oblivious to irony. The term allowed Travis and Andi both to believe they were the mentor — however reluctant — in the relationship.

Andi moved her lips but nothing came out. The problem with Travis' question is that it always left her at a loss. Even though she knew it was coming. She refused to give it the time it required. To come up with a response was to show she cared what Travis thought and the one comfort she had from the whole relationship was that she did not.

Travis looked at Andi's blank face and again sighed internally. The woman had no sense of humour. That's what her problem was. Sure she had all sorts of other problems but — and he praised himself for his insight — that was the one problem all the other problems boiled down to.

'So how goes it, Andrea? Buddy.' Travis' lips puckered on the 'B'.

'Andi.'

This too was part of their ritual. Andi knew Travis thought that she was using a boy's name in a man's world but that actually was her name. If anyone was to be held responsible, it was her mother since she couldn't imagine her father having played a role.

'Sorry?' she asked now.

'Sorry, what?'

'Sorry, what did you say?'

'I didn't say anything.'

'I thought you did.'

'I didn't.'

'I thought you said a man's world.'

Travis looked surprised but didn't say anything more.

After a moment he sighed again — aloud this time — turned and flagged down Cathy. Watched her approach. Her every step. Not even trying to disguise it. Cathy arrived flushed. Like she had just run up the steps or someone's husband had copped a feel at a party.

'Well, well, well. Travis here would like to order.'

'And what would Travis like?'

'How about them flapjacks with a side of bacon. Or make it the bacon and eggs with a side order of flapjacks.'

'The Hungry Man's Meal?'

'Always. Hungry.'

Cathy left without taking Andi's order.

'Do you have to do that?'

'Do what?'

But Andi wasn't sure. Ogle the wait staff? Refer to himself in the third person?

'Talk as if you were from Texas.'

'I don't do that.'

'Flapjacks? Who in Toronto says flapjacks?'

'Well, apparently, I do.'

He looked at her challengingly. This was the closest they had ever come to saying what they really thought. Normally Andi just sat there smile, smile, smiling until Travis' teeth ached from the effort of watching her. He felt a thrill course through him. He didn't want the feeling to end.

'I'd like to make it with one of the waitresses but it's bound to end badly and I hate to get bad service. I come here too often.'

'Pardon?'

'You heard me.'

It was nice to see Andi put off balance. With her glossy, dark hair — chestnut or some other word people probably used for it — her trim physique. He imagined hours in a yoga studio. Flat-chested but he was OK with that. It made her clothes hang better. Travis noticed these things. People thought he didn't but he did. He saw that she was displeased and he couldn't help but think that it was with him even though she looked that way from the moment they first met. It made him feel angry and protective at the same time.

'Don't you get tired of the bullshit?' Andi asked.

Hah, now they were getting somewhere.

'What bullshit? I would like to make it with one of the wait staff. Well, maybe not Cathy. Too eager.'

Andi's expression almost made up for all those times she had made him feel selfish for being a few lousy minutes late.

'That bullshit,' she said. 'Why are you telling me that bullshit?'

'I'm just making conversation.'

'People just making conversation talk about the weather, hockey, the quality of my coffee or the lack thereof. People just making conversation don't talk about screwing the wait staff.'

'We both know what the weather is like. I don't watch hockey and I couldn't give a shit about your coffee, or the lack thereof.'

Cathy showed up with the Hungry Man's Meal and a coffee, which Travis passed to Andi. It made her inordinately happy, which saddened her. She always suspected that she was overly susceptible to small acts of kindness. How little it took. Far too little. She reached for the cream to hide her embarrassment. She struggled to open the small plastic pack.

Now what, thought Travis. He wanted to reach over and take the cream from Andi and open it for her. To prove capable in this small but not pointless task. That's it. To be useful. That's all he ever wanted. Someone had robbed him of this. He couldn't remember who. Possibly his wife — his ex-wife — but he couldn't be sure.

Andi gave up on the cream. The coffee was cold. The cream would have only made it colder. This, whatever this was, had to be put behind them. Travis was a work colleague. Her 'buddy' no less. It would never do. Not even remotely. No, they had to do more than put it behind them. They had to pretend it never happened.

'You don't watch hockey?' Andi smiled. It was an effort but she smiled.

Travis smiled back.

Andi was taken aback. Travis had never done that before. What was he doing?

What had he done now? Andi looked frightened. Eyes wide, body pulled back. Christ, you'd think he had said something offensive.

'Ah listen, Travis, about this 'buddy' thing. I know the firm wants us to do it and all, thinks it would benefit us and therefore them, but I don't think it is. I mean benefiting us and therefore them, so I am sure they wouldn't mind if we, ahh, just stopped seeing each other.'

Andi smile, smile, smiled throughout this little speech making Travis' hair hurt, and he saw with sudden clarity what Andi was. She wasn't sleek, well-dressed and successful, a pay rank ahead of him. Yes, she was all those things, too, which was kind of sexy in a 'I can handle it' sort of way but what she really was, was dissatisfied. No, not even dissatisfied. She wasn't a ball-breaker; she was bitter. One of those bitter girls. He had met them before. The type was familiar.

It was hard to tell at first through the designer fashions and the shiny hair but she was his wife — his ex-wife — in disguise. Even though they looked nothing alike — Yvonne was soft and blond, while Andi was all angles from her slightly asymmetric bob to her pointy shoes — they were exactly the same. Travis, now that he saw it, couldn't believe he hadn't seen it before.

He knew. Andi would have felt like she hadn't asked for much, a house — no a 'home' — love, support and — what was the word that Yvonne had used? — constancy. And men would have failed to deliver. Somehow they were always failing to deliver. No, she hadn't asked for much, no more than what many women managed to achieve the world over, or at least fifty percent of them, but she had been denied even that. And her dreams had been so small.

The realization that Andi was, well, nothing special, was a release.

Andi smiled again. Why was Travis making this so hard? He looked positively put upon when all she wanted to do was make it easier for them. For both of them. Well, really just for her. She didn't care about him but he too would benefit from this selfish act. Surely he could see that. Instead he looked sad. Why were men like that? So incapable of stepping to the plate, sucking it up and just getting on with things. Why did they have to be so sensitive? She could see it in Travis' whole body, which for once was angled towards her. And then she saw it.

He was a failure. Yes, he had been called upon and had failed to make the grade. She glanced to where she knew a wedding band probably once resided and it was suddenly easy to imagine this womanizer married. Her: believing herself to be unassuming, undemanding. Him: ready to provide, to do things, change light bulbs, clear the drains, to be the man. Her saying he needn't worry. It was OK. It was fine. She'd just call a plumber. Her with the kids, clinging to her knees. Him ultimately unnecessary. Yes, that's what Travis was: dispensable. It was almost enough to make Andi feel sorry for him.

Instead it released her.

'Andi.'

Travis looked up at her. Andi hadn't realized she had stood up, was pulling on her coat, scarf, hat, gloves. Winter, it made quick escapes impossible.

'Gotta go, Travis.'
'See you next time?' And Travis smile, smile, smiled.

As the light of the last of the falling stars faded, you shifted your body, but you didn't get any closer to me. It was quiet and we were silent, letting the darkness envelop us. And just as I began to relax, to forget, to feel the comfort of solitude that happens only when I'm not alone, you spoke.

'What do you always wish for?'
'Release.'

The Fighter – Anahera Gildea

I killed him with a gun, in his sleep. I couldn't have got close enough
with a knife to take him out — he had the muscles of an old fighter
and the grimace of a bull dog — that's what I thought of as I yanked
the trigger. I look at my hands clamped now onto the front of the
dock, big and flat like paddles. I'd have liked to have punched him to
death, bone to bone, but I wouldn't have won.

I know my lower jaw juts forward and I have teeth missing.
That's what I'm supposed to look like, eh? Like I've had a hard life?
That woman with sixty four years on her, five kids and twelve
grandchildren. Bet the media is lovin' it there in the gallery, watching
it all play out. If I was allowed to read the paper I'd be fuming 'bout
the way it's all going down. How racist it all is. I know I'm not well
groomed, but nothing can remove the majesty of these ancestral
bones standing here against gravity, against time, against man.

They don't introduce my iwi and I don't offer it. I just look at no
one and answer the questions. They convicted Lindy Chamberlain on
the fact that she didn't show remorse but I can't fake tears for
anyone, least of all this lot. They'll head home to their rightful place
in the middle class tonight, chuffed that they've done their civic duty,
but for now they're all just holding their breath. There's one guy
who's clearly got whakapapa. He's in his forties, clean-cut, fancy hair
and casual suit. Casual like you wear it every day, not like you just
borrowed it or had it dragged out of mothballs for this big event.
Casual like it's normal. Bet the lawyers like him. All the others are
gonna turn to him when they get in that little jury chamber to decide
if it was premeditated or if I was reacting, caught up in abuse and
shit.

This room smells like sweat. It's engrained in the seats. As if the
room has a plague of desperation and hate. Of rage and futility. Or I

could be making that up. It could be just a room that at the end of each and every day gets disinfected and sprayed and wiped and sprayed again. Still smells. I wonder how many stomach ulcers have ballooned in this room? How many tears have stained the wood of the chairs, and how many fingernails have etched their own tiny carvings on the undersides of the seats as loved ones, and frightened ones, gripped their bases.

My boy has been here the whole time, silent with his arms folded on that puku that's lipping over the belt of his jeans. Every now and then I see him wriggle his nose and sniff, twitches it sort of, or snorts — that's where all his emotion is — that's where he's doing all his words. I'm watching him and I know he's busted up on the inside. He's never gonna forgive this mother. Never. But he's looking after that wee bub there; our little moko, soft face and big eyes, clutching that peach-faced doll that never has no clothes on. I can see its plastic face from here but everything else is made of cheap calico. If the doll had some clothes on you'd never know that. You'd never see that the stitching is all coming unstuck neither, and that someone who's shit at sewing has tried to sew a leg back on with blue cotton. But that girl loves it. Like she loves her Nan.

I've a good mind to get over there and give that son a telling to. What the hell does he think he's doing bringing a child in here, granddaughter or no? It's bloody ridiculous. He needs a good kick up the arse.

But I'm not allowed. I'm here listening to the private business of this family gone wrong. Here in this cavernous room where the ancestors on the walls are peoples we've never seen before. We don't know them. I don't know them. They're up there taking the time like that giant clock that's ticking.

Auē, that lawyer is saying years of abuse led me to it. His thin magician's nose is angled into the sun and his words are perfectly customised to this space and this audience. He is saying I couldn't spend any more days with him.

'Why didn't you get help?'

'Why didn't you leave earlier?'

I stayed for the kids. I hate the sound of my voice when I say it. Like how I hate listening to our answer machine, my answer machine, at home. Some strength there.

But there's not much of a case. They've got photos of the crime scene and it's bad. It's all blood on the bed sheets and brains on the wall. I didn't cover him up or touch anything after; I just called the police and sat there with him, waiting.

In the photos you can see our bedroom. Where we slept, and fucked, and talked, and where the kids crawled into bed with us when they were small and scared. On the drawers next to the bed is an older picture — of a younger me — when I was seventeen. Faar, I look mean in that pic, hot as. If I picked it up and held it next to the wrinkled and broken tooth version I am now, I wouldn't reckon they were the same. The one in the photo looks like she came from a 1950s movie. And the photo looks faded even, like it has been whitewashed for some effect; slightly coloured over to take the richness out of that young girl's skin.

I see you there in that pic, I say, standing there like you're at the prow of a great ship. I see you, and he saw you too. So that every time he fought you, or stuck himself in you, he would've had to look across and compare you then to the gnarly assembly of muscle and bone that we two had become.

I put on a little make-up this morning and some good clothes, tidy and clean. But I didn't wear my pounamu. I left it on the shelf in the cell. Those who knew me would have noticed that detail. They would have commented on it for sure. It was my thing to wear it. Like a beacon or a signifier.

When they called out Josephine Hammersley, I stood up and admitted it all just like that. I've never given up anything so easily before in my life. What a lark. Murder was a big deal, not a thing for office workers sitting on the jury in their suits. Not a thing for women taking notes who had their own grown kids and tane. Not a thing for a student who kept a mind-your-own-business, second-hand sort of lifestyle, seeing his parents when they were in town.

'She did it, she's admitted guilt.'

'Everything now is simply a formality for the jury.'

'Josephine Hammersley killed a man. In cold blood. She was awake. She got a gun. She stood over him, and killed him. It doesn't get much simpler than that.'

'Were you there?' I yelled. *'Were you fucking there? How do you know for sure? There were circumstances. Extenuating circumstances.'*

'There were extenuating circumstances. Abuse.'

They couldn't prove it. None of the witnesses could prove that. No one ever saw him lift a finger to me. Except that boy of mine and he wasn't reliable.

'It is reasonable that Josephine would have exaggerated the circumstances.'

'None of the other kids' testimonies said she was abused.'

'She was dissatisfied with her life.'

'The jury is only required to make a decision based on evidence.'

They hacked away at me.

'It's not up to a jury to decide if Mrs Hammersley experienced abuse or not.'

'End of story.'

'End of story.'

'End of story.'

But by the time they get to that jury room I reckon there'll be no one holding up consensus in the deliberations. No one will be sitting there unable to say why this violent woman might be a victim and not a criminal. No one will oppose a verdict of guilty, super guilty, mega guilty — of premeditation, of evil, of brownness, of poverty, of all the ills of society rolled into our one bedroom, on that one night.

Within the hour they are back to me. Me, without my pounamu, the woman who had killed her bastard husband with his face like an angry pug.

So I nod my concession and don't look over at that mob of do-gooders or the foreman standing up to speak for them, for me. I look over to my boy and his kōtiro sitting there with that doll, all trussed up and broken. My moko's face, as the verdict is read, is turned up to her father, to see his expression. Both of us wahine watch him snort, watch the set of his jawbone and his nostrils flare like a horse whose heart is pounding and pounding with swollen blood, as me, his mother, presided over by the Right Honourable Justice Stokes and a bunch from round the neighbourhood, is sent down.

She raised her forearm to defend herself, defend her face more importantly, cos the face is impossible to hide from others. Bruises there invite questions and judgements that she had no interest in entertaining. Her sharp protests and the coarse tearing of her clothes were the only noises. He said nothing.

With every cry she made he smacked her again. She never tried to get away but let him grab her clothing, ripping it until she was wearing nothing, until she was naked and head down and then he raped her. It was his thing. Once she was quiet, and clothes-less, and subdued, he would turn away, repulsed.

He regularly took his hands to her: whipped her good. That was his right when the wife was disobedient. And his particular hands had a knowing — a way to feel when to stop hitting and when to start again. A gift he reckoned, an ability to judge — in the reaction of her body, in the speed with which her defences went up — where on the continuum of going too far they all existed.

The Leaping Place – Vivienne Joseph

My husband cannot believe I want to hang-glide off the mountain but he is trying very hard to understand.

'Why?' he asks. 'Why now?'

I think of saying, 'Because I'm not dead yet.' Instead, I offer, 'It's not really a mountain. It's an extinct volcano.'

He collapses forward with his hands, his head, resting on the steering wheel of our car.

'It's only a little volcano,' I say, 'two hundred and thirty-two metres high. I've done my research, looked up the accident statistics.'

'And?'

'Only minor injuries.'

'Minor?'

I can hardly get the words out for laughing. 'A sheep or two were flattened.'

He thumps the wheel. 'For God's sake!'

No, I think, for *my* sake. 'D'you know, I've never had a broken bone? In all my thirty-three years — not so much as a broken pinky.'

It's not really about broken bones. Bones don't haunt my dreams the way those sad-eyed children — our promised future family — do.

He looks at me and shrugs. 'So?'

'Don't you see? I've never pushed the limits — not even when I was a kid.'

'That's no reason to take risks now.'

'That's *every* reason.'

'I don't understand, that's all. Not for the life of me.'

'You'll have to stop feeding me amazing lines.' I pat him on the arm. 'You know I just have to say, it's for the life of *me*.'

I see the beginnings of a smile, a sweet smile and it melts my socks, as my grandma used to say.

'It's something I want to do. Like you did that time. Remember *The Human Fly?*'

The smile disappears and in its place, genuine astonishment. 'What?'

'You do remember.' I keep the triumph out of my voice. 'We were at that pub in Wellington, you know, out by the airport.'

It's weird, but as the memory comes back, I can actually *smell* the pub, hear the ear-shattering music the noise level compounded by the tidal pitch of many disparate conversations. One moment we were watching and the next, he was handing me his beer and jacket, pulling on the ridiculous fly suit and grinning like some schoolboy performing a dare.

I'd shrunk back into the darkness of an alcove, clutching his jacket and beer, feeling — what exactly? Not just embarrassment.

He turned at the last minute, looking for me and I saw the puzzled expression when he couldn't see me, saw the way he hesitated before turning once again and then running straight at the wall where, assisted by two men, he managed to affix himself — thanks to the tenacity of Velcro — to the board half a metre from the floor.

He'd hung there, giant antennae quivering, like someone or some *thing* I did not recognise any more.

Even now, so long after it happened, I still don't know whether to laugh. All I can remember is the fear I felt at that moment, real and frightening — rubbing itself around me like a cat.

I wrap my arms around my shoulders. The car is heating up but I feel chilled. 'Why did you do it?'

He squirms, frowning now. 'I was drunk. End of story.' He runs his hand through his hair. 'You're not — tell me you're not doing this to pay me back?'

'Of course not. I was just mentioning the fly thing because I thought it'd help you understand why I want to do it.' But I can see in the tired way he shakes his head that we are on different trajectories.

Reaching out suddenly, he circles his arm around my shoulders.

I snuggle back and close my eyes. 'Did you ever have a dream of flying?'

'Nope — not that I remember.'

'When I was a kid I used to have this same dream, night after night. I'd be outside somewhere and I'd just give a little jump — the way you see birds do it — then I'd be in the air flying. I've never forgotten that wonderful feeling of swimming through air, through clouds and how everything below seemed so small.' I breathe out. 'The colours, the smells, the air lifting me — singing through my body.'

'A kind of out-of-body experience?'

I fight it but can't control the giggle. 'No, but I can't wait for the real thing.'

He's annoyed now and withdraws his arm; sits hunched. 'I'm not laughing,' he says.

I pat his arm.

He shrugs my hand away and turns, but not before I see the wetness in his eyes.

'The real story, the *unfunny* story, was that every morning after I'd dreamed this, I'd go outside and try to fly. My mother caught me once preparing to leap off the garden shed with a sheet tied around my shoulders as a parachute.' I make a silly joke to myself, about being 'grounded' by my parents afterwards, but don't pass it on. 'I grew out of it. Eventually.'

'And now — now, do you think hang-gliding off this extinct — *small* — volcano, will help you recapture your childhood dreams? Is *that* what all this is about?'

I look at my watch because I can't think of a truthful reply, if I even know what is true. Or if there is even anything true left in this world. 'It's nearly eleven.'

He pulls the key out of the ignition and opens his door without speaking.

As we walk past the Norfolk tree beside the car park and towards *The Mount,* as the locals call it, I reach for his hand, which he does not pull away. It makes me think he's forgiven me, at least, for now and frees me to chatter.

'This place has a split personality, don't you think?' I ask.

'In what way?' He pulls a face. 'If, that is, places have personalities at all.'

I point left. 'Over there, the water is calm and boats rest easy.' I point right. 'While over there, we have wild surf, rips and danger.'

'Tombolo.'

I squeeze his hand. 'I love it when you talk dirty.'

'No.' He sounds irritated. 'I think that's the geographical name for the way the spit links the mountain to the land.'

We walk around the base of the mountain and along the sandy path with the sun hot on our backs and I hear the seedpods of gorse popping and the distant seagulls' cries. The air is warm and carries the smell of salt and baked grass.

The path steepens beneath our feet and I have to stop to catch my breath. Descending walkers pass us with 'Hullos' and 'How're you going?'

He is discreet about shortening his stride so that I can keep up. From time to time I can feel him giving me quick sidelong glances, checking to see if I'm all right.

I think it's funny how love is in the selective details, the smallness of daily life. They are the minutiae we mourn when someone leaves.

At the summit we stand and look down at the perfect double curve of the surfing beach below.

I don't say it but when I turn my head seawards, it's the curve of wings, I see.

'We'll glide down and land on Main Beach,' I say.

It's windy and I can feel the tug of what are surely powerful thermals. For a moment, I wonder at the need for wings of any kind.

'Cape Reinga's up there somewhere,' I say, pointing north.

He turns his head and we both look into the blue of distance.

'The Maori name is Te Rerenga Wairua,' he'd read from the brochure as we stood with the other tourists at the lighthouse. 'It means 'the leaping place of spirits'.'

I loved the belief — that after death the soul travels up Ninety-Mile Beach to where an eight-hundred-year-old pohutukawa tree clings to a cliff. There the soul leaps, beginning a long journey back to the ancestors.

We'd looked down at the tree, hanging above the war of surf and swell far below. Wondering at the faith shared by roots and rock, a faith that defied both gravity and disbelief.

'You're not Maori,' he says at last, as if reading my thoughts.

'I know,' I say. But I don't tell him about the strange feeling of exhilaration as I think about souls leaping off that cliff. The final turning to wave goodbye at Three Kings Islands.

My husband hugs me and brushes his lips across my cheek in a chaste, small-boy kind of way as I wait by the hang-glider. I notice the tremble in his body as he holds me.

After the diagnosis, I remember wanting someone to explain to me — my parents, my husband — the facts of death. If we do possess a soul then how does it leave the body? And, with the recall of an embarrassed eleven-year-old, through which *orifice*? Or, is it attached like a shadow to our heels? Have we been incorrect talking so arrogantly of the *soles* of our feet?

Peter, the instructor, straps me into the tandem harness. On the back of his jacket is the company's logo 'Fly Like An Eagle'.

'Ready?' he asks.

I smile easily. Lately, I've learned what a smile can do.

Peter explains, again, what to do and what not to do. How we'll use our weight to direct the hang-glider. How we'll fly along the coast then turn and look for dolphins. 'They're dream conditions today,' he says.

As we run towards the edge I remember reading about bumble bees and how some scientist would not believe they could fly until it was scientifically proved — this despite the millions flying around him. I think it all comes down to what we believe and what we know is true. What I want to believe is all around me now.

We leap off the edge and, as Peter has warned me, the hang-glider dips down more than a metre. I scream but it's lost in the ocean of air.

Is this free falling how it will be? Leaping off, leaving all worldly things behind, letting go. Entering freely into the unknown territory of the spirits? I'm laughing inside, a little crazy, as adrenaline asks the question: 'flight or fight?' I choose, of course, *both*.

The lift, when it comes, wrenches my head, my heart, skyward. My breath is sucked from my lungs and each gulp I take to replace it seems like making a fresh, somehow absolved, beginning.

'You okay?' Peter yells in my ear.

I show him the thumbs-up and try to look back at my husband but my head is forward and my body seems at the whim of forces without pity.

The hang-glider flies and hangs as it's supposed to. We see dolphins dipping far out to sea and black-backed gulls flying upwards in a thermal below us.

I try sorting out what is true and what is not.

It's like my childhood dreams and it's not. The smells, the colours, the land and sea painted below are the same, but I am not. It's flying like an eagle and it's not. No self-respecting eagle would groan as the hang-glider does each time we change course.

This is also not like the moment of my death, my soul embarking on its last search for peace.

It's more like a joyous, heart-strong leap into life.

These Last Desires – Wes Lee

Violet called her husband Peter into the bedroom. 'I want you to make sure they get my hair right in the coffin,' she said.

He stared at her, a tea towel slung over one shoulder, a wet, soapy wineglass in his hand that dripped onto the carpet. 'You're only fifty-nine years old.'

'They didn't get my mother's hair right and I don't want that happening to me. Tell them they have to shampoo it and just leave it to dry without using a hair dryer. I want it to look natural.'

'Those kinds of things don't matter.'

'They matter to me. That's why I'm telling you now. Don't let them put any kind of gel in my hair … or lacquer,' she shuddered.

'I don't want to think about you like that.' He turned and walked back out to the kitchen.

'Well, one day you might have to,' Violet whispered.

Her mother's hair had not looked right in the coffin. They'd swept it back from her face in a stiff, grey pompadour instead of letting it fall naturally across her forehead, lightly skimming her eyes, the way she'd worn it in life. At the time, Violet had thought it was a good thing that they'd got it wrong. It hadn't looked like her. It had made it seem possible that her mother could be somewhere else, not lying there, so final in the coffin.

'It's not her,' she'd told Peter, 'she's not in there anymore.'

She'd wanted to reach out and brush the hair back over her forehead but it had felt as if it would be an intrusion in that very public place, like suddenly reaching out and adjusting a stranger's clothing on the bus. And there had been too many people trying to hurry her away; to move onto the next leg of the journey, back at the house with the finger food waiting, the napkins and the silver.

The next stage.

She remembered turning away from the coffin, walking through the still, dust motes of the funeral parlour, fighting the overwhelming desire to run back and throw her arms around her mother. To never leave her. To never leave that place. All the rituals, the structure, the hushed sense of decorum was probably a good thing she thought — it kept relatives from jumping into graves.

The wrong hairstyle had been a kind of blessing. It had made it easier to distance herself from the reality of it. It had helped her get through. But later, when the images had come back unbidden — her mother's mouth set in a strange, grim line; her hair so stiff and lacquered like a pale, pasty version of *Little Richard* — she had known that her mother would not have liked being seen that way. Her mother had prided herself on her grooming, she'd set her hair each morning in large rollers and brushed it into long, loose waves.

She should have taken a photograph to the funeral parlour so they would have known how her mother wore it. But in that blistering state of shock she had not thought about how they would style her hair in the coffin. It had been the furthest thing from her mind. Nobody tells you those things. Surely it should be standard practice, she'd thought later, that they should ask for a photograph. But they hadn't said anything. And then it was too late, her mother's hair had been how it was and Violet had tried to rationalise it — *there* in the parlour — so it wouldn't seem so painful that her mother had been overlooked.

'It's Sod's law,' her mother would have said, 'shafted … even in death.' She had always had a ripe sense of humour. Women were most particular about their hair. What might appear to be a minor detail to a man, could be a major crisis to a woman. Her own hair had always been difficult to manage: thick curly ringlets that most women envied, but had caused her a lot of heartache when she'd tried to style it in any way other than a bob. She had found a way to control it after a lot of trial and error. The best way was just to shampoo and rinse and then leave it to dry on its own so the curls would spring back naturally into place.

Hairdressers always wanted to tame her hair; to blow-dry it straight, or apply product to it. That's what they called it — *product* — as if it was this nebulous, brand-less thing; a magic cure-all.

Snake Oil.

She'd wanted to give Peter a photograph to take to the funeral parlour in the event of her death. They were both at an age where they could conceivably pop off at any time, and anyone could have an accident. But could she trust him to do it? Would he sidle in and not be forceful enough with them? He had always been unwilling to face things. Maybe he would be so numb with grief, and shuffling in a catatonic haze, that he would not think about the task she had given him. This last thing she wanted. She imagined pinning a list of instructions to his coat like a child.

Even if he managed to hand it over, how could she be sure that the undertakers would get it right? If she wrote out a list of instructions would they follow it? Hairdressers never had, so why would undertakers? The best thing was to catch it early; to speak to someone so they'd know what she expected. She'd seen television programmes where people pre-selected their coffin and talked about the music they wanted, so why couldn't she talk about her hair?

Did it seem so strange these thoughts, these last desires?

Each morning, when Violet exercised the dog, she walked past a funeral home. She had wondered more than once if that's where she would end up, or Peter, *god forbid*, before her. It was strange how we travel past these places, the hospital, the funeral parlour, and never really think that one day we'll be in there. Lying in a bed with tubes coming out of us, or on a metal table ready to be sluiced and sliced; emptied and filled with chemicals. All the things that were waiting to be done to us. All the strange hands that would (one day) touch us. *Awaited us.* Strange fingers that would peel back her clothes and look at her. Not in the forgiving way that Peter looked at her — aware and oblivious at the same time to every mark, every scar — but with a cold, unfeeling eye.

Barkers Funeral Home: it was a cheerless place, a breezeblock, 70s structure that had been originally painted white, but over the years had become a pockmarked grey: lace curtains unmoving in the windows, nothing twitching behind there. A silent, implacable building; the kind of place that if you moved closer and peered through the glass you'd see dead blowflies on the window ledges, caught in the fringes of the net curtains. She'd never leaned in that close, but she knew they'd be there, tiny bodies tangled in a sea of white nylon.

Barkers — it was too close to *barking mad* for her liking. It was a grotty little place, and she supposed a few people had ended up there who'd had no say in the matter. With its brightly painted sign it looked like a second-hand furniture emporium. All it really needed were flashing lights: *24 Hours — We Never Close.*

She didn't want to end up at Barkers.

She'd seen an advert on the television for a funeral home located over in the Wairarapa — *The Wilson Chapel of Rest.* The camera had panned along a driveway that curved up through expansive grounds. A comforting male voice had extolled the beauty of the landscaping, as if the prospective clients would get to stroll amongst it. At the end of the driveway, a stainless steel fountain shot multiple jets in front of an ultra-modern building. Its wide, glass foyer had looked like the entrance to a four star hotel.

Violet searched Mr. Wilson's clear, hazel eyes. It was impossible to see what he was thinking. He was like a doctor, you only ever saw one tenth of the iceberg floating on the surface. Too many secrets burgeoned underneath.

He had greeted her in the foyer, a slim elegant man with a dry, firm handshake. He'd moved her quickly through to a bright, white room that seemed to contain an overabundance of office machinery. A fax machine continually clicked into service, dropping creamy sheets of paper into a plastic tray. A state-of-the-art computer took prominent position on his glass-topped desk — a facsimile of *Planet Earth* pinged from one corner of the screen to another. There were none of the clichés of the cloistered undertaker's office — dark mahogany; heavy, velvet drapes — the *too solid* paraphernalia that represented generations who had tended the dead.

The soft buzz of technology underpinned the silence.

'My mother was not presented in an appropriate way,' Violet said.

'Surely not by us?'

'It was in Dunedin … she died suddenly. There was no time to ask what she would have wanted. No one even told me to bring a photograph. They made a terrible mess of her hair, it was a travesty.'

'We always request a photograph of the loved one.'

'What if you can't replicate the hairstyle?'

'We have a professional hairdresser on staff who is able to replicate any hairstyle.'

'What if the hair is difficult?'

'What do you mean?'

She got a flash of a woman holding a bottle of shampoo on TV, pressing it against her cheek, extolling its virtues with a blinding, white smile on her face.

'I like it to be done a certain way. I can't rely on my husband to remember, he's a good man, but he might not be okay on the day and he won't listen to what I want now. He doesn't want to think about it.'

He smiled. A neat, precise smile.

'We will make sure that you appear as close as possible to your photograph.'

She knew she'd been trying to find something human in him; behind the remote gestures, the perfunctory smiles. It was just like all the other encounters she'd had with professionals of any kind. Falling back on their practised routines to keep everything smooth, so that nothing could burst in and splinter the banality of the moment; push in and shatter it. Not even death.

71

She stared around his antiseptic office. She wanted to see something out of place, something untoward — a spider's web floating down from the ceiling, a blowfly spinning on the window ledge. She wanted to see this dapper, little man tackling some out-of-control mourner to the ground as they wrecked havoc, a primal grimace on his face. She wanted to see him burst into flames.

'I don't want you to use any gel, or fudge, or hair spray. I don't want to look like a trussed-up clown.'

'I can assure you that everything will be taken care of.'

'You'll find the instructions written on the back,' Violet said, as she passed the photograph over the desk.

When Violet made her way out through the gleaming foyer she saw that the door was open to the parlour. She peered inside the dimly lit chamber. The air felt very still. *Deathly still*, she thought with a wry smile. The kind of stillness that is almost supernatural. The kind of stillness that is not experienced anywhere else.

The shiny black coffin beckoned. It was difficult to look at anything else, even if your eyes were drawn to the flickering candles or the faux stained-glass windows for a brief second of respite, the coffin dragged you back. The focal point. The incontrovertible object with its one grim purpose. The glowering black box.

She remembered the money box her mother had given her as a child — a black, tin coffin with a wind-up key. When she'd placed a penny on the lid, a compartment had slid open and a gnarly, skeletal hand had risen out of the coffin to scoot the penny inside. Such a glorious, wicked thing to give to a child. She'd shivered with delight each time that hand had appeared, raking over her penny. The lid snapping shut as the coin disappeared.

The coffin in the parlour was surrounded with flowers, the kind of flowers that people choose for funerals. Nothing bright or sexy — waxy bloodless flowers: *straight-jacket cream; cold arctic white.*

Violet approached the coffin. That's what people did —

approached — as if they were creeping up on something, trying not to make any noise, as if they were afraid they'd alert the sleeper inside.

It was an old woman.

Of course, Violet thought. It wouldn't be some *James Dean* look-a-like, a matinee idol, replete in his perfection. Someone she could gaze upon and drift into a reverie about the fullness of his lips, the strong line of his jaw; the appalling, youthful waste of him.

It was an old woman, with fat, mottled arms and liver spots on the back of hands that had seen too much dishwater. Her red, sausage fingers had been threaded together, crossed over her chest; a gold band buried on her wedding finger. A plain-looking woman resting after a life of sacrifice. Her poor, sad sack of a body sinking into the padded satin, the way it had sunk into the last bed, the last chair that had moulded its shape around her.

The woman's hair looked outrageous. Surely it was wrong. So stiff, as if they'd sprayed a tin of lacquer, rigid and unnatural. But perhaps that's the way she'd worn it. Perhaps she had given Mr. Wilson a photograph of the 60s bouffant that she'd held onto throughout her life.

Violet hoped that he had understood her. That she had gotten through to him. That he would get it right.

Her mother had told her that her own hair had been very curly before Violet was born, and soon after it went straight. A kind of transference had taken place; the bright, springy curls that had belonged to her mother had become hers after her birth. Her mother had always told the story in a cheerful way, not a hint of resentment that her hair had gone straight. She had always loved Violet's hair. She had taken great pride when strangers had commented on it.

What beautiful hair your daughter has.

It was one of the stories that would be lost now that Violet didn't have a child to pass it on to. *Your grandmother's hair turned straight when she gave birth to me...* She knew with a sharp, sad jolt that the story would die.

If Peter had wanted a child, would there have been the same kind of transference? Would her hair have turned straight if she had given birth? It was too late to think of things like that now. The choices had been made. She stared at the woman lying in the coffin. She wanted her hair to look the way it had looked the last time her mother had seen her. She knew that no one would ever look at her again in that same way. Not even Peter. She remembered the last gesture that her mother had made — pushing back a strand of hair from Violet's eyes, appraising her just before she prepared to leave the house. Her mother moving towards her, touching her fingers to her face.

'There,' she said. 'There now, Violet.'

Making Room for Music – Vivienne Ball

Genevieve is out for her morning walk through the bush. Her dog, Beethoven, is on the end of his lead, pulling at it, wanting to get ahead. Genevieve is feeling in a leisurely mood this morning and is dreaming a bit about life. She is wearing her favourite linen trousers with a long flowing tunic, and remembering the many countries she has visited and her varied work overseas.

After many years away she is now back 'home' and kind of settled. Kind of. She's pleased to be living near the bush and thankful for this small city that allows her to own a villa not far from the outdoors she loves.

She can hear the ripple of the stream that is off to the side of the path, and the birds calling their good mornings to the world. Gurgle, gurgle, gurgle from the tuis, and in the distance a bellbird sings. Along the track are ferns, lancewoods, the larger ngaios, and a totara. She is enjoying the walking, and the taking in of the refreshing air. It is clearing her mind and she feels a little exhilarated.

She leans on the rail that overlooks the stream. Beethoven does not want to stop and is tugging again at the lead, but she wants to lean on the wooden fence for a moment and look into the distance. It is a scene of trees, hills and valley. Taking several breaths, she relaxes and enjoys the gentle breeze on her face.

But soon it's off down the path again and on to the street. Then she is undoing the gate leading to her home. There is a small garden inside the front fence and at this time of year it is overflowing with an abundance of colour from the many flowers she has planted in her herbaceous border — roses in a profusion of pinks and reds, and some annuals in unusual purples with plenty of white to offset the colour. It reminds her of the English countryside she particularly enjoyed while on her overseas sojourn.

She's expecting her old school friend, Cecile, later. Dear, organising, practical Cecile. A true friend. Genevieve dusts around the blue and white china she bought in England and France, taking time to gaze at her prints and sketches bought from artists in the streets of France and Italy. Her books are a bit untidy and she stacks a few back into their place on the shelf. She had been looking at her gardening books the night before, searching for ideas on developing the messy, uncared for piece of section at the back of the house. Rhododendrons and azaleas are a possibility, and they would work well with some native trees. Also amongst her books, collected over the years, are some biographies of musicians, some pictorials from places she has visited, and a few books about writers. *The Brontes of Haworth* falls from the pile she has just picked up. That was bought on a visit to the Bronte Parsonage Museum with a writer friend.

Better check the fridge. There are the olives and some cheeses she bought on the drive with Cecile the previous weekend. On the bench is a bottle of olive oil, locally produced from trees growing in the place where there used to be sheep farms. Who would have thought it? She has a nice bit of ham and some salad ingredients. But she needs some fresh bread. She can leave Beethoven inside while she pops to the local bakery and maybe has a drink at the same time. It's great having the bakeries and cafes so close. Another change that has happened in the years she has been away.

After buying the French bread at the busy deli, she settles at a table on the sidewalk. It has turned into a most beautiful late summer day; warm with a slight breeze. Ah, she loves the warmth, the feeling of summer, and it seems to be going on forever. Better than last year she has been told. Her Earl Grey tea comes in a white china teapot with a blue lid. At the table next to her sits a well dressed young couple who seem to be discussing something of a business nature. Some runners come past, followed by an elegantly dressed woman with brown trousers and gold coloured blouse.

She takes a sip of her Earl Grey. Last night's dream is haunting her. She'd had trouble sleeping and the heat had kept her awake. She had eventually dropped off to sleep but all too soon awoke with a fright. In her dream she had left her new home for a walk. A walk-about of huge proportions. When she returned to her house, it was flooded. The water was over a foot deep and continuing to come in — rising rapidly. She was helpless. In her dream her friend, Cecile, had come to help her.

She'd forgotten to use the strainer and found in her tea a kowhai flower which she pulled out with the teaspoon.

Back to her thoughts. 'Helpless.' That was how she felt in the dream and it is weird how a mild but helpless feeling has been welling up in her, underpinning everything. A helplessness underneath the beautiful summer experiences, the excitement of her villa and her satisfying friendships, her job, and her many experiences travelling the world. It is weird that she actually feels helpless, because on the outside she's OK. The sun is beautiful — amazingly strong, and the sky is blue with just a few little clouds. Two young women walk past — one with a modern red patterned dress over black tights. The other in white summer trousers and sixties style psychedelic orange top.

There were things she had put off with her travel and her work. They had engaged her attention completely. Now that she is back home, it is as though something deep inside is saying it is time to take a new direction, to nurture her long-hidden talents. Now she has no excuse. And she knows what it is. For her greatest desire is to get a piano to learn to play. She thinks it is a silly idea, but it will not go away. When she was in Carnegie Hall she heard the most magical pianist and ever since, she has wanted to learn. There are obstacles in the way — for a start, there is not much room in the villa. Then she wonders if she will have time to do it properly. There is the cost. She doesn't have a lot of spare money, having just bought her villa.

Picking up her bread in its brown paper bag, and her floral bag, she knows it is time to head home if she is going to get lunch organised in time.

Cecile arrives in her usual bright and cheery way. They enjoy a cup of locally roasted coffee and talk about travel. Cecile has just come back from a trip to the West Coast and is full of it. The funny thing is that Genevieve, in spite of all her travels, has never been there but listening to Cecile thinks she would like to go.

But the real news is of Cecile's planned overseas trip. This is no small, just planned-off-the-top-of-the-head trip; it is the trip of a lifetime. Cecile has unusual interests, and luckily her husband shares them. History buffs, Cecile and her husband are off to America to follow the route of the early settlers going out west in their wagon trains. Hearing her friend's excitement, Genevieve is touched by a feeling of jealously. Not for the travel, she has done plenty of that, but because Cecile is fulfilling a long held ambition.

It's this talk of a long held ambition that makes Genevieve feel brave enough to share her own thoughts. Still slightly fearful of what Cecile will think, Genevieve tells of her long-held desire to play the piano. There had been other musical interests in the past and always the attending of concerts — something she enjoyed overseas and particularly enjoys with friends now she is back home. She thinks the practical Cecile will flatly say there is no room for such a thing in this nice, but small home.

But Cecile takes a different tack, immediately taking up the idea and making suggestions for where the piano can be fitted in. There is the bay window — a bit of unused space in front of that — but then it might not be good for it to be in too much direct sunlight. What about the hallway? There is actually room there and you could have a little heater with an extension cord. But she really does think a corner of the lounge would be best. Then they could join up and have singsongs with friends. Oh, she likes the idea immensely and it seems to grow on her. She really thinks her friend should follow through with this. It feels right. She would have them out shopping for pianos this very afternoon. And the teacher who taught her children — she taught adults as well; but then again, maybe someone more advanced, because even though Genevieve has not played the piano before, she has been to lots of musical events and has sung in choirs so perhaps one of their contacts would know of the right person. Or the piano shop might advise.

It is fortunate Cecile has to head off soon to another commitment as Genevieve is really a bit out of breath with her enthusiasm.

Genevieve hums some of her favourite tunes as she tidies away the dishes and picks up a few things from the lounge. Wandering through the dining room she picks up a brightly coloured grape from the large bowl of fruit on the sideboard. A couple of stray books are put on the sideboard in the bedroom alongside her travel journals. Those journals are precious, kept over the years and full of memories, stories of people and places. She remembers what she wrote after she visited Carnegie Hall. The magic of hearing a famous pianist and the uplifting exciting atmosphere.

As evening draws near she decides to take a drive. She has been drawn to a riverbank. To a particular part of the riverbank. The sun sets and it's a clear night — the night sky is ablaze with stars. The sort of night you feel an awareness of the whole universe. You feel small, but not insignificant, an important part of the Whole.

At times like this she feels full of memories. Memories of her childhood, friends, the dreams and the daydreams she had as a small child.

It is now that she comes to the gate, the beautiful wrought iron gate, the same gate that has always been there. The street light shines on the roses that line the drive and there is a light on in the lounge. How she misses that lounge. Not so much for the room itself, though it was always comforting and going there was like going into a cocoon, to retreat from her life in the outside world. As an adult it was always that room she had in her mind when she thought of 'going home.' But it's not just the room; it's the conversations she misses, her father sitting in an armchair by the fire, lighting up his pipe and reminiscing. There were the family gatherings that took place in that room, and always the piano, her mother playing by ear, many different tunes.

She can hear the singing and the laughter. Always there was music. Except for the year her father, a doctor, decided to put his local practice into the hands of a locum and take them all to a third world country where he worked in a health clinic. And then it wasn't so much music, but a whole world of experience opening up. She suspects that was what led her, and her brother and sister now working in remote places, to travel.

She thinks of her dream of last night. Of being flooded. In the dream she had to work her way out of the water. And as she looks over the river to her childhood home, she feels enveloped in a peacefulness rather like a cool balm. It calms the rising uncertainty she's been feeling, and the wondering if the life she's living is the life she really wants to live. She starts to feel a strength rising, bringing a new dimension into her life and into her future. She puts Beethoven in the car, for he has come with her. She hadn't wanted to leave him at home on such a beautiful evening.

Back home, she picks up one of her musical biographies, gets out the sheet music she inherited from her mother, and thinks that with a bit of furniture shifting a piano could fit quite nicely into the corner...

The Great Balance – Jo Randerson

I've never been able to sense things, to feel things before they happen, but I have heard that some people can. I've heard of folk who can see people's deaths ahead of time. They say they see shadowy fish scales on those bound for drowning; white shrouds and crucifixes on those due for disease. Loving couples, joined by radiant threads, find them severed when one partner dies, leaving broken strands reaching confusedly up towards the sky, searching for their lost complement. Ever disappointed. Ever seeking.

But me, I see none of these things. My mother used to swing pendulums to foretell the future, but I never saw much in that. I do believe in some sort of destiny, fate even, but I don't see how you could know it ahead of time. There would have to be some sort of cross-time communication channel for this to work. If it's taken us centuries to develop cell-phones and the internet, it seems preposterous that there's something faster and more efficient that can actually go into the future as well. Something which connects information directly from head to head without wires and without microchips? If you believe that, then you probably believe in remote healing and transcendental meditation. You probably believe in prayer.

Nevertheless, I did once experience some kind of fore-knowing, only once, when I first met Dave. I saw him from behind, just the back of his legs leaning over a car, and I knew he was the one. I just knew it. I hadn't even glimpsed his face, yet he was radiating some kind of aura that told me *this was it*. I could have walked past at my usual pace and he would have missed me, but instead I slowed my walk just enough that when he raised his head, he saw me, the bright crimson and red of my jacket and the exact shape of space I carve out on this planet. I didn't have to do anything else, I just made sure he saw me and left the rest to fate. And that's how I've learnt to do things: you just put yourself in the right position and trust the rest to the universe. Things can go wrong if you try too hard.

I was right to trust the universe.

I never told him this, but while we were talking together on that first day, an image flashed in my head of the two of us, grey-haired and smiling, rocking away on a porch. I saw the pale peach of a wedding dress.

And the reason I question *the knowing* is that how could some people's knowing be so different from others? If I *knew* that he was right, how did so many of my friends know he was wrong? It wasn't so much what they said, but what they didn't say. I knew marriage was a big deal. I knew that you had to be sure to make a commitment like that. I knew that when people said, 'It's your choice,' they meant, 'You're making a mistake.' There was only one person, one, who actually said, 'I see bad things in this marriage,' and she felt so embarrassed afterwards that she apologised every time she saw me until things got so awkward that we had to stop meeting. On our wedding day, she was conveniently absent, which she was, of course, profusely sorry about, and she's remained sorry ever since. I doubt if I'll ever see her again.

Anyway, we were married, Dave and I. And the years flew by, as years have a habit of doing. And I was pleased to discover that we were happy, really truly and radiantly happy, despite the trends around us. We were alarmed at the rate of relationships collapsing amongst our friends: affairs blossomed, divorce was rife, nasty weeds grew over previously idyllic marriages, and each party refused to bend down and pull them out at the root. With every late-night phone call, each heart-broken friend showing up with a bottle of wine and a puffy face, I felt even more affirmed in my choice. As I lay in bed each night, I quietly thanked some entity that Dave and I had each other, and dropped off to sleep feeling wondrously, deliriously lucky. Such happiness as I'd never expected. I knew we'd be together for always, that this bond was too golden to be broken. But I would never say that out loud, as I didn't want to curse it. Not like I cursed that boy back in high school, and that's a thing I never want to talk about again.

I'm not sure everyone could survive Dave's lifestyle. I've heard others say they couldn't cope with the constant fear: the repeated trips away, my anxious waiting at home, his unquenchable thirst for the depths. I know other wives have struggled in my place, but I always want to ask: have you not seen the pictures they bring back from that nether world? Those magical, dimly lit places of ambient green and blue, the gentle wafting of plants and animals, the dark cavernous blacks and the cold emptiness of muted life? The nothingness? The silence? How could you stop someone who returned from such trips so energised, pulsating with life like he had plugged into some sort of spiritual battery charger? How couldn't some of that, even just a little of that enthusiasm rub off on me? I never tried to stop him going.

And there've been many things said, that near-death experiences make you live more vigorously, and that freezing a flower bulb makes it leap from dormancy into ferocious bloom. There've been all sorts of theories on men who like high-risk activity: they're re-living childhoods, refusing to grow up, searching for meaning, whatever. But I think it was simpler than all of that: it was just something that Dave had to do. It was in his nature to risk everything, and who can argue with nature? How can you argue with something that calls you like that?

The mother of the boy who died, she saw it differently. She said we each had a certain amount of emotions allotted us. She said if you used up all your Happy early on, then you would have some Sad coming to you. Likewise, if you had too much Sad as a child, say your father got killed in a war or your mother went crazy from heartbreak, you would have some Good Things coming to you in your old age. And that was what drove you to do things sometimes, an urge to right the balance somehow. She didn't call it fate, she called it 'The Great Balance'. It sounded like a reasonable theory, but it didn't really fit my experience. Because nothing very bad ever happened to me, so how did I end up with this happy life I have now, when others I know have had horrible childhoods, and then gone on to have horrible adult lives, far worse? It's all very well to talk of The Great Balance, but I've seen lots of people with much more Sad than seems fair, and likewise some get a lot more Happy than they really should. I mean, if that's the way it works, then who is in control of that distribution? Is the person in charge of equilibrium perhaps sleeping on the job, could they be slackening a little in their duty? Because it doesn't seem like there's much equality going down. But maybe you get the hand that you can deal with.

She told me about that day, the day that he died. More specifically, I asked her to tell me. I thought I should meet this woman whose son Dave was going to bring back. Everyone knew the story of the boy who went down too far and never came up. Everyone knew how dark and remote that journey was, how unlikely the chance of return. There's something about a place so unforgiving, or maybe something about that small window of possibility, just the tiniest chance of survival, that dares one to beat the odds. The fact that so many others have failed. Dave was always attracted to this. Did he think he was somehow superior to the others? Or, beneath it all, was he actually seeking death, but too scared to admit it? I know this world lacked some warmth of meaning for him. Perhaps that final boundary held the only promise of resolution.

Whatever the reason, Dave had gone down to see for himself. I don't know exactly what he was looking for, but he found something: the boy, floating calmly in the inky, endless night. I don't know what happened between them. Perhaps the boy spoke to him in some way, showed him something, made him an offer. Because when Dave came back, something was different. Like he had looked something real in the eye and it hadn't looked away.

'I'm going down again,' he said. 'I'm going down, and I'm bringing him back.' Probably the most dangerous dive he had ever attempted, to one of the deepest and darkest abysses on the planet.

Probably the riskiest and bleakest destination you could choose, with the least likely chance of return. As I say, how could I stop him? How could anyone stop anyone doing anything?

'You can't change the future and you can't change the past. Hell, you can't even change the present,' said the old lady, the dead boy's mother. 'All you can do is observe it differently.' She had never liked him diving, but he told her he was going to do it anyway. Said he was grown-up. Said it was his choice.

The first time the boy went, he had quoted someone; 'A life lived in fear is a life half-lived.' She answered, 'A life lived in the kind of fear that you put me through is a life two times lived, three or four times lived, and that's at least one time too many.' Because the greater depths are the ones we plummet to back home, waiting for the phone call which will send our world spinning apart in several directions. The phone call that will hack an enormous hole into our lives which can never again be filled.

'He told *me* about fear,' she continued. 'What fear did he know? If something went wrong, if he had an accident, his adventure would just continue on into a new and uncharted zone where he would never have to think of us again. What had he to be afraid of? What would he be losing?'

I wondered where that place was exactly, and how he felt now, and if his relationship to fear had changed. They say you should confront it, fear. Although I think there may be a difference between standing in front of the dog, confronting it, and actually poking a stick in its eye, daring it to bite you. I know for a fact that dogs bite back. Their nature demands that they do so.

I asked her about the phone call.

'It began with a dark rumbling, in the early morning. A feeling was growing, an increasing pressure beyond my control. It was intensely hot, mid-summer. About 4.15 in the afternoon. I was sitting outside, right here in this very chair when my toes went numb. All sensation in them disappeared, and I thought it must be something to do with the heat, thought I must have heat stroke or something.

Everything around me instantly softened, as if everything was melting. I was looking at the leaves on the oak tree, and the shadows they cast on the grass, and then the colour slowly started to drain from the picture. Everything went grey. I went grey. The shadows and the leaves merged together, like the ground was flowing up into the sky, and the sky was draining downwards into the earth. Things were going where they should never have gone. The universe had reclaimed all its pieces, for some mysterious audit. Then someone was tapping me on the shoulder. The colour came back, the leaves parted themselves from their dark likenesses and everything returned to its rightful place. But not all my pieces returned. I felt it absolutely: something had been taken away that would never again come home. A dark emptiness had been carved into the landscape. They had given me back a hole where there should have been a piece.'

We sat outside on her porch, while I gazed at the shadow of the oak tree, the very one she had sat beneath that fateful day. To me the leaves were clearly distinct from their shadows. The colours were clear. The ground was below me, and the sky fixed firmly above. And despite the heat, I could feel all parts of my body, even my toes felt alive and awake. I waited. As I said, I know not to push too hard.

After several minutes she spoke again.

'This was before the phone call. I lifted myself out of the chair and walked into the house, over to the bench, where I made a cup of tea. I was still in a daze. The tea was cooling on the bench when the ringing started. Of course I knew what it would be. I never did drink that tea. I haven't touched that cup since.' She waved her hand at a cup on the bench in the kitchen, and we went inside to have a look. There it was, that same cup of tea from seven years earlier, a brew that had never been touched, never enjoyed. A brew that had brought no relief. We stared at the layers of green and brown mould, some kind of mystical garden. The smell was not as bad as I expected. Still, I was amazed what had grown from some boiling water and a few leaves. 'Everything grows something,' she said. 'Even from nothing, something will grow.'

I pondered this on the way home. When I arrived back at the house, I tried an experiment. I hid an empty pot in the garden. 'Let's see if something will grow from that,' I thought. As I stood there, thinking of the pot full of nothing, I wondered if I could cope with losing a son. It's hard to know what you can cope with until it happens. Don't women lift trucks and trains off their children pinned beneath? I should have asked if she had a happy childhood. Did she think she brought about his death by too much Happy as a child? Was the universe trying to even things out?

I was glad Dave was trying to help her. Although if I lost someone close, I wouldn't want them home seven years later. Trapped under the water all that time. Bones. Rotted skin where the wetsuit clung tight. I think he might have preferred to lay there for eternity, in the cold dark silent nothing. There are moments in my current life when that seems like a pretty enticing place. Away from all this noisiness. Away from the bright lights and changes. Away from the emptiness. At these times I want dreadfully to talk to my mother. I want dreadfully to find that pot I planted and see if anything ever did grow.

And for Dave, it became all about numbers and distances, metres and minutes. It wasn't about fears and premonitions, it was plans and charts, tests and hypotheses. It was safety measures and calculating variables. It was equipment. It was dive shafts and oxygen balances. It was a new kind of mouthpiece.

And the day before finally came, and then the night before came. And the night before went. And then it was *the day*, *that day* came, and so Dave finally went. He seemed calm enough, although his skin seemed odd to me, slightly cold and pale, slightly clammy. Slightly fishy. And who knew what the outcome would be. Not me. I had no pendulum to predict the result. I had nothing. Just a belief that people make the best choices. And why on earth did I think that? That old lady had got me thinking a lot about Balance, and fairness and unfairness. Why some things happen, and why others don't.

And I have to say, some strange kind of unfamiliar sense came over me, on that day, as I sat there waiting for the news. I think it is fair to say that some funny things started to happen. I had decided to stay behind, as I got too nervous near the action. And I knew that round about now, there should be some sort of news. 'All well, Dave on the way up, has the boy with him.' Or, 'Didn't go all the way down, problems with the crank shaft. Will try again tomorrow.' Or 'Lost contact, but line is still moving. Assume all well.' They usually keep me up to date. And I didn't feel worried at all, not in the slightest.

So I went to sit outside, out under our huge jacaranda. And I thought about that old lady, and I thought of my mum, and I thought of those bulbs that bloom into life. And I thought of how some people know, and others don't, and how others *might* know but are unable to stop themselves.

And at the moment, I noticed a strange sensation in my feet, like the heat was draining out of them. They say he was breathing too fast. They say he should have relaxed, taken his time, not pushed quite so hard. But Dave was obsessed, fixated on freeing the boy. And he did free him, so on one level, he succeeded. The boy came home to his parents, that waterlogged pile of bones and flesh whom they had loved and cared for so tenderly. That promising brew that nobody ever drank. That investment that gave no return, or maybe it did, depending on your view of an empty plant pot.

And as for Dave, he came home too. Not immediately, but several days later, he came home to me. But he had changed, really changed, and none of us could deny it. He had made the one fundamental change which we all must make, but when? I keep asking myself, when? How can we know when?

And as I sat there waiting for him on that day, I was asking the universe why certain things happen the way they do, why some people get Happy and some get Sad, how some people want to do things that hurt them, that hurt others. I was wondering what kind of plan that is, and who was responsible for what seems like a pretty randomised pattern, because you can call it Fate, or Karma, or God's

Will, but as far as I can see it's just pure chance, and I would give all the Happiness I ever had in childhood that loved ones would never have to be separated. And as I sat there wondering this, I saw the leaves on the trees begin to pale, and then merge with their dark counterparts on the ground. Everything became one for a moment, then one piece was removed from my puzzle. I saw things going where they should never have gone. And when things started separating again, I stood myself up, as if in a trance, went over to the kettle, and switched it on. I put a teabag in the cup, and I waited for the phone to ring. And I saw coloured threads reaching up towards the sky, that from this moment on would be eternally searching, and eternally disappointed.

The Greedy One – Rachel Marr

As the first rays of sun shot across the Indian Ocean, Skyla, a cliff swallow, opened her small bright eyes and blotted her ears against her chicks' insistent squawks for breakfast.

One chick in particular, Jaslin, made a great display of holding her white and brown flecked belly and rocking from side to side. 'I will surely die if I don't eat soon, mother. Quick, quick, fetch my breakfast.'

Placing a kiss on each of her four chicks' ruddy, scarlet cheeks, Skyla perched at the edge of their bowl-shaped clay nest and scoured the vertical cliff face. No one from her colony had come forward to be her mate since the recent death of her partner; she would have to feed her chicks alone.

Soaring into the air, Skyla caught a thermal current and circled the coast line for hours, her thoughts only on her chicks' survival.

At last she returned to the nest and dropped flies, mosquitoes and lacewings into her chicks' open throats. 'There, there my babies,' she cooed, 'now you can sleep and grow into big, happy swallows.'

As Skyla began to settle into the cramped nest for a short rest, Jaslin began to squawk again. 'I want more, Mother. You gave me the smallest mayfly. It's not fair. Daddy would have given me more food. I'm starving.'

'It is not true my dear,' said Skyla as she patted her chick's downy head, 'I love you all equally.'

Jaslin did not hear her mother's soothing words and continued to complain and cry. 'I hate you. I will cry and cry and cry, until you feed me more.'

Rubbing her salt-stung eyes Skyla remained firm. 'But my dear, the currents are too strong today, I will get very tired, and we don't have Daddy to help anymore.'

With a shrill screech that made her siblings wince in fear, Jaslin flung her head back and opened her throat. 'I will not stop until you get me more food. Now!'

'Make it stop, Mother,' whimpered Eima, Peta and Toowar, 'please, we beg you.'

Skylar wiped away the tears from her three gentle-natured chicks and flew away from the nest. She had to manage her brood alone now, and if feeding Jaslin more food was the only way to placate her, then that was what she would do.

For many days Jaslin continued to demand of her mother. To keep the peace, her mother continued to spend hour after hour flying across the exposed coastline in search of enough food to satisfy Jaslin's insatiable appetite, and to feed her other hungry chicks.

Desperate to obtain food closer to home, Skyla began to raid other cliff swallows' nests.

Even when her mother arrived home, dejected and bleeding from fighting her neighbours for their hard earned food, Jaslin turned a blind eye and relished only in having a full stomach.

On the eighth day, as dawn broke, Skyla remained in a deep sleep. Her body was battered, bruised and exhausted from the endless hours of flying and battling.

'Look what you have done to poor Mother,' Eima said to Jaslin. 'She is so weak; death could take her at any moment, and all because of your greed.'

Jaslin scowled at her sister and continued to preen and admire her vibrant and healthy metallic blue wings. 'It is not my fault she struggles to find food. I didn't ask to be born.'

Jaslin had grown plump and was almost adult-sized compared to her thin, less well-fed siblings. 'If you weren't such a fool Eima, you'd be as plump and healthy as me, silly sister. At least I get what I want.'

Eima cowered away from Jaslin and put her small wing protectively over her sleeping mother.

As the morning turned into midday the sky rolled and darkened with storm clouds.

Unsettled, hungry, and feeling vulnerable, the three siblings, Eima, Peta and Toowar, huddled against their mother for warmth and tried to sleep.

Jaslin watched her siblings with contempt. 'At least I will not starve if Mother does not wake up,' she said to their motionless forms. 'I bet you all wish you had been as clever as me, don't you?' and without another thought she fell into a deep sleep.

High above Skyla's nest, a female sparrowhawk from two cliffs away, flew in a series of fluid circles. *Yes*, thought the sparrowhawk with a smile, *the family of swallows are asleep and completely unaware of my presence.* It was a rare day that a cliff swallow, let alone a whole family of cliff swallows, remained asleep while a sparrowhawk was nearby. She knew that cliff swallows were, by design, very alert and fast prey.

The sparrowhawk narrowed her bright yellow eyes and dived.

As the hawk neared the cliff that housed Skyla's family, the surrounding colony came to life. Cliff swallows evacuated their nests and flew in all directions. Their loud squawks of warning woke Eima, Peta and Toowar.

Deep within Skyla's subconscious, an alarm bell rang. Her chicks were in danger. She opened her blurry eyes and felt a heavy shadow fall across the nest.

Skyla knew it was too late for action.

The hawk dived the final few metres towards the nest, turned mid-air and descended with its yellow, wiry claws towards Jaslin's sleeping form. The sparrowhawk wrapped its talons around Jaslin's stomach and rose into the air again. *My, my*, it thought, *this is surely the plumpest cliff swallow along the entire coast line. My chicks will eat well tonight.*

Skyla and her remaining chicks watched in horror and disbelief as the sparrowhawk disappeared into the oily sky. Even when the sparrowhawk was no longer visible, they could all hear its satisfied cackles reverberating through the heavy clouds.

Shine a Light – David Mason

I've blocked this out for years, you know. And it's worked, more or less. I can go weeks, months even, not thinking about it. Still, it never really goes away. Lately it's been giving me hell. This pain slowly burning through me, like smouldering coal in a ship's hold. Open the hatch and it could ignite. Much better to keep a lid on it.

Lately, I've been thinking about what this bloke told me one time. He said if you want to forget, you got to shine a light on it first. It gets all mean and ugly hid away there in the dark. A bit of light does wonders for seeing it the way it really is. Seemed like such a bad idea. I mean, I know the way it is and I don't want ever to see it again. But the thought won't leave me alone. Now there's these two embers burning in me. There'd always been this pull in me to go back. Couldn't see the point in it. What would I do? There's no one there anymore. Just all this bad shit. But I just can't stand this pain any more. So I'm going home. Take the lid off it. See what happens.

I like how this old Titan runs. Not much younger than me, but she can still lay those miles down. Will you look at that now? The whole Waikato stretched out, far as the eye can see from below these Bombay Hills. We're definitely on our way now. Auckland at our backs and that green carpet all the way down to the lake.

With the steady throb of the engine and gentle curve of the road my mind drifts off to our old place on Cameron's Line. I got four brothers, two older and two younger. I can hardly remember Steve and Rick being at home. So it was mostly Allan and Johnny, always called 'the boys', and me.

It's hard to figure what to shine a light on. Maybe it's my Dad. I didn't know other boys didn't get the crap beaten out of them all the time. That's just how it was. I never could pick when it was coming. He'd be all matey and fun, laughing and going on about how we were proud, tough descendants of gold miners come up from Central and then I'd be back-handed to the other side of room. Or it would be one of the boys. Mum got a lot of it. We all knew it was our fault. Shouldn't speak in that way or look at him like that.

Bike's suddenly dropped to one cylinder. I stop and check the points' gap with a bit of cigarette paper but she's set fine. I pull the plug. Ah, look at that, a tiny stone chip. That'll be it. I clean it and screw the plug back in but no luck. Not even when I fit a new one. Shit, I'm snookered.

The old girl runs rough on the one cylinder but we struggle into the motor-camp just to the north of Taihape. It's late Saturday so we'll have to wait it out till Monday morning for the bike shop to open. Maybe this is telling me not to go on. Maybe I'll just go home on Monday and skip this whole stupid thing.

Lying in my sleeping bag here thinking. I could go home. It's not far to the old house. What am I scared of? The memories are getting stronger and more of them are tumbling in the closer we get.

I remember how Mum went to hospital for a while and Dad was around home more, but he was hopeless at the job. He burnt the food and us boys did what we pleased even though there were a lot more beatings. I was scared without Mum around. When she came home, I took to seeing that she was alright, making sure the two boys didn't get under her skin too much and helping with whatever I could. Every night I'd check that the house was locked up real good. We didn't see much of Dad after that and no one ever talked about what Mum did that day.

Sunday and I'm bored. I decide to check the faulty side of the bike with parts from the good side. I work my way right through the system till I get to the points again and there, in the gap, is a tiny bit of my cigarette paper. Well, bugger me, how stupid was that? Lucky I found it before taking it to the mechanic.

I pack up and get on the bike, feeling good about sorting it out on my own. Good enough to keep going. There's nothing to be scared of. I get a coffee and a bite in town and we're out on the road, engine running sweet as.

Not far short of Bulls, I take the road through Feilding and out onto Cameron's line.

It's a lifetime since I've been here but there's no doubting how to find the old place. She's a sight. Front windows all smashed and the front door hanging by the top hinge. I pull the handle and the door just falls on me. I step inside and wait for my eyes to adjust. Yeah, I remember this place. Still the same old smell. The smell of family and living, fish and chips and beer, Dad's fags and smoke from the coal range, all rolled into that indefinable, familiar smell of home. Here, on the left is the living room we hardly ever used and right opposite is Mum and Dad's room. The hallway still has that flintlock-pistol patterned wallpaper that always got me thinking of Long John Silver. Ah, we had some fun in this hallway, playing cricket and bowls and hide and seek.

There's the boys' room next to Mum's. Jeez, what a mess. Someone's been sleeping here. There's a stained and tattered mattress, beer bottles, bits of clothing and crap. Actual crap. Some arsehole's had a shit in the corner.

And here, right next the loo where I could hear every fart and piss, is my room. My room. Holy shit. What a rush of feeling. All these memories and images are just leaking out all around. There's my bed in the corner. No mattress on it now but you can see where I scratched my name in the paint. I remember doing that. When I couldn't stand the yelling and fighting and sickening moans as Mum took another fistful from Dad and the pillow over my head wasn't enough. Yes, that's when I cut my name in there, as if to say, 'This is me. Here I am. And when I get big I'm gonna do that bastard.' I can just about see me, all curled up there, face to the wall, so full of hate and frustration and fear. And so small. Such a little kid, full of all that torment. I wipe the tears from my eyes.

I get a feeling, like someone tugging on my coat, urging me, telling me, 'You think this is bad. Come look at this.' I'm pulled to the end of the hallway with the flintlock wallpaper and the black telephone hanging off the wall. A part of me seems to know what's coming, doesn't want to know and can't stop it. It's all foggy like a dream and it seems like I'm being dragged by this little kid who's saying, 'You gotta come see this. You gotta see this with me. I can't do it on my own anymore.'

We're standing in the kitchen. That burning in me is so hot I can't take it. I know what I've got to see, what I've got to put some light on.

The kid, holding me by my jacket, says, 'There. Over there in the corner by the coal range. That's where we found her, didn't we.' He looks back at me, pleading, tears streaking his anguished little face. 'Look. You've got to look.'

I look. And remember. I remember that picture from so many years ago.

She was in the same tired green and black dress she always wore. Standing on her toes in her pink fluffy slippers, her head cocked to one side and her eyes staring at nothing. There was a line of blood at the corner of her mouth. She was doing a slow pirouette like a dancer. She'd told me, one time, she'd been a dancer after leaving school. Right off I'd thought she was dead. I don't remember feeling anything much. Just interested seeing mum standing on her toes slowly turning around. I can see her now, clear as, twirling on that rope. I'd stood on the chair and cut her down with a kitchen knife and her body slumped to the floor. I remember thinking it was a shame to interrupt the dance. I'd loosened the rope from round her neck and she gave the most amazing rasping gurgle, sucking in pretty much all the air in the kitchen. I wiped the trickle of blood with the corner of her dress and watched some colour return. Then another of those awful air-sucking gasps. You could see the focus come back into her eyes, trying to steady the image before them. They'd gone from seeing nothing to seeing me.

'Hullo Jimmy,' she'd rasped. 'You back from school already?'

Then she was quiet for a bit, the light in her eyes fading in and out as she slowly gazed around the room. She'd turned back to me with a sad little smile. 'Sorry about all this,' she'd said, gesturing with a sweep of her arm. 'Here, sweetheart, give me a lift up, will you.'

I sag to the floor in that bare, dark, deserted kitchen, the shadow of the kid lingering at my coat hem. I can see him. I can feel what he felt. The thought struck me hard in the chest, if I can't handle this what must it have been like for him, just an eleven-year-old kid? I hug my shoulders and cry for that boy, and for me too.

Death at Twilight – Frances Cherry

On that first morning in the retirement village, Judith woke up to a banging in the apartment next door. She looked at the time — 5:28 am. What on earth was Mrs. Armitage doing? Judith knew her; she'd been introduced to her when she was first shown the place. Mrs Armitage, Glenda, was a frail-looking woman with brown weathered skin and white-peach coloured hair — probably red at one time.

Perhaps she was in trouble, had fallen and was calling for help? Judith rolled out of bed and went to the wall to press her ear against it and listen. Nothing. Then it started again. Judith picked up the phone and rang the office. No answer. Surely someone was on duty in a place like this? You never knew what could happen to some frail old person.

Judith sighed and put on her dressing gown and slippers. Then she strode down her hallway, unlocked the front door and stepped over the low wall onto Mrs. Armitage's lawn. She went to her door, knocked and called, 'Mrs. Armitage, Mrs. Armitage, are you all right?'

There was no answer, but the banging continued. Judith knocked louder and called again.

A voice from across the driveway hollered,' What's all the racket? Don't you know the time?'

Judith turned and saw a man hanging out of his upstairs window. 'I'm sorry,' she said as she moved closer so as not to disturb others. 'I could hear banging in Mrs. Armitage's, I thought she might be in trouble.'

'At it again, is she?'

'Sorry?'

'This is a frequent thing with her, don't you worry about it. She's all right. Probably in some fantasy about her life on the farm. She was a farmer's wife at one time.'

'Oh, I see.' Judith frowned up at him. 'It *is* rather annoying.'

'You better get ear plugs, love. That's the only answer.' He closed his window.

Ear plugs, she thought. Bloody ear plugs. What have I come into? I thought places like this would be quiet. She stomped back into her own apartment and poured water into the electric jug. May as well have a cup of tea, she'd never sleep now.

She sat out on her patio, cup of tea and toast on the small wooden table in front of her, and stared down at the rolling lawns and the lake where ducks floated. It was a beautiful place this Twilight Village, though she hated the name: it was so depressing. She was a fit woman of sixty-seven and hoped she had plenty more years left in her yet. There was nothing wrong with her at all, she was fit and healthy, but having lived next to those noisy young people in the city, she'd decided a place like this was the answer.

Now she was retired she wanted to write. She'd always had a hankering to write crime novels, and having worked as a senior secretary at Police Headquarters she'd gathered lots of ideas. A quiet place where someone else looked after the lawn and maintenance of her property was now definitely the answer.

There were no children and no husband to worry about, although she had been married for a short time, years ago, but unfortunately he'd turned out to be gay, or homosexual, as the term was then. Nice enough chap, they still kept in touch. She was a sensible woman; people had said that about her all her life. But she had to be, she had to think forward, be prepared for any eventuality, just in case. There was no-one else to rely on.

This place had a large dining-room and bar where she could have a meal and a drink if she wished, also a tennis court, swimming pool and small gymnasium, but she had no intention of using any of the facilities. She would cook for herself (she liked cooking) and go for long walks by herself. She liked her own company; other people could be a trial.

She had everything she wanted here. Two bedrooms, one of

which she'd use as an office. She didn't need a room for guests because no-one would be coming to visit. Her lounge was reasonably spacious and had that lovely view through the large sliding glass doors. She had her television with its big flat screen. She had her stereo and books.

There was still some unpacking to do, she'd put on her old clothes and do that before she had a shower.

She hummed as she made her lunch and then stopped. The sound of a television began blaring from next door. You'd think it was right here in her own room. She could hear someone saying, 'I'm glad your mother's dead, she was an evil woman. You *know* what she did to me.'

Judith marched down the hallway, out the front door and over to Mrs. Armitage's place. She bashed on the door but of course no-one came: the silly fool was obviously as deaf as a post. She went around to Mrs. Armitage's french doors and knocked. Through the terylene curtains she could see the back of Mrs. Armitage's head as she watched the television. Judith knocked louder. Mrs. Armitage didn't move. Judith pulled at one of the doors and it opened. She poked her head through and bellowed, 'Mrs Armitage.'

Mrs Armitage clutched her chest and swung around. 'Oh my goodness, you gave me such a fright.'

'I'm sorry.' Judith signalled for Mrs. Armitage to turn off the television.

'It's my programme,' Mrs. Armitage said. '*Emmerdale*, I'll talk to you later.'

Judith strode into the room and switched off the television. 'Mrs. Armitage,' she said, 'I can't hear myself think because your television is so loud.'

'What's that?' Mrs. Armitage cupped her hand behind her ear and pushed it forward like a shell.

'Your television,' Judith said, loudly and precisely. 'It's far too loud!'

'Eh?'

'Your television. Too loud. It's driving me mad.' She spoke as if she was talking to a child.

'Eh?' And then Mrs. Armitage seemed to process what had been said. 'I haven't got it too loud, it's just right.'

'What you need,' Judith said, trying to sound friendly and kind, when what she wanted to do was attack the stupid woman, 'Is earphones.'

'Don't like them,' Mrs. Armitage said. 'Hurt my ears.'

'I'll get you some really good ones.'

'How much?' said Mrs. Armitage.

'Don't worry, I'll pay.'

'Oh,' Mrs. Armitage said, as she aimed the remote at the television. Of course it didn't go on and Mrs. Armitage looked puzzled as she attempted a number of times to get out of her chair.

Judith stood in front of her and held up her hand. 'Mrs. Armitage.'

'Call me Glenda,' Mrs. Armitage said.

'Glenda, I'll put your television on again and then this afternoon I'll go off and get you some really good earphones. Do you promise to use them?'

'I'm not a child,' Mrs. Armitage said.

'No, of course you're not.' Judith said. 'It's just that I get migraine headaches if there's too much noise,' she lied.

'Oh dear,' Mrs. Armitage said. 'My sister used to get those.'

Judith turned the television back on and left.

After Judith had finished her lunch (with torn pieces of softened tissues in her ears) and washed the dishes she went through into her garage and got into her car. As the doors rose up she could still hear Mrs. Armitage's television, now on to another programme.

When she was home again everything was quiet. Perhaps Mrs.

Armitage was having a sleep. She'd better not go in there until later. The longer she slept, the better.

Then she heard a light tapping at her door. Mrs. Armitage come to apologise, perhaps? When she opened the door, there was the gentleman from across the road. He was an upright man, smartly dressed in a black jacket and grey trousers, a maroon coloured cravat tied around his neck.

'I've just come to see how you're settling in,' he said.

'It's not been easy,' she said. 'I've just bought Mrs. Armitage some earphones,' and she told him how loud the television had been.

'She won't use them,' he said. 'Many before you have tried, including her own family.'

'Oh no.'

'I was just going up for drinks,' he said. 'Would you like to come with me?'

'No thanks. I prefer my own company.'

'Oh come on,' he said. 'Come and meet some of the others.'

'I'd rather not.' She felt herself backing away from him. 'I came here to be quiet and write.'

He laughed as the television next door came on again. 'You'll probably find it much more peaceful up there than down here.'

Judith sighed. 'I'll just go and get my handbag.'

As Judith and Bob headed up the driveway to the administration block where the restaurant and bar were, they were joined by others who were all dressed up as well. Bob introduced her to them — Eva, Emily, Connie, Betty, Marcia and one man, Henry. Bob told them about Judith's problems with Glenda and they all laughed and said what a pity Judith had happened to buy the apartment next to Glenda because she was a one, that one.

Bob directed Judith to a table by the window and insisted on buying her a drink because he was, she could see, a gentleman from the old school.

'I'll get the next one,' she said.

'We'll see,' he said.

She looked around to see others, sitting around tables, talking and laughing. This isn't my world, she thought. I don't belong here, I'll shrivel up here.

'Why aren't the apartments soundproofed?' she asked Bob.

'I thought they were,' he said.

'I think I'll have to get someone in to investigate what can be done because I can't put up with that racket. I came here for peace and quiet. I have work to do,' she said.

'You said you were a writer?' He leaned forward.

'It's nothing.' She waved her hand as if to dismiss him.

'Romance, is it?'

'Certainly not. It's a crime novel.'

'Ooooh,' he said. *'Interesting.'* He looked at her with renewed enthusiasm, which was the last thing she wanted.

The builder came and lined the walls with acoustic tiles which, of course, made the lounge and Judith's bedroom a little smaller but they more or less did the trick. Sometimes she could still hear the hint of noise.

So the problem was solved in that area but it wasn't as far as Bob and some of the other residents were concerned. Bob was forever coming over to offer help or ask her for a drink or a meal. Sometimes she relented to keep him happy but not too much. Others knocked on her door at times to see if she wanted to play bowls, or go for a walk. They all called her 'the crime writer' and were constantly asking what she was writing about. If only she hadn't said anything. When visitors arrived, Judith was introduced as 'Judith, our crime writer.' But the thing was, now that she had the time she couldn't think of anything to write. She sat at her computer for hours trying out ideas and then deleting them.

One morning she heard someone banging on her bedroom

window. She sat up, her heart thumping and turned on the bedside lamp. 3:57 glowed on the clock radio. Who on earth was it? Then it happened again: knock, silence, knock. Was it louts from some of the houses around about, trying to scare the elderly and infirm? She jumped out of bed, went through into the lounge and opened the french doors. There was Mrs. Armitage, in Judith's newly planted garden, swinging her stick around like a blind person.

'Glenda, what are you doing?'

'It's time to milk the cows,' Mrs. Armitage said. 'I was looking for the path. I can't find it.'

'Glenda you're in a retirement home. There are no cows to milk.'

'Where's Charlie?' Mrs. Armitage said.

'Charlie?'

'My old fellah. He's always rushing ahead of me.'

'Glenda, you need to get back to bed,' Judith said. 'Come on, I'll help you.'

'Charlie, Charlie,' Mrs. Armitage wailed. 'Where are you, Charlie?'

'Come on,' Judith said, trying to take her arm.

'Leave me alone,' Mrs. Armitage cried and swung her stick around, whacking Judith on the shoulder.

'That hurt,' Judith yelled.

Torch lights swept across them. Bob was there, as well as someone else — one of the women Judith had previously met. For the life of her, she couldn't remember the woman's name.

'What's going on?' Bob asked and then he said, 'Oh,' when he saw Mrs. Armitage.

'She hit me,' Judith said.

'Off to milk the cows, was she?' the woman, whatever-her-name was, said.

'Come on, Marcia,' Bob said. 'Let's get her back to her bed.' He grabbed Mrs. Armitage's stick and handed it to Judith while he and Marcia got on each side of Mrs. Armitage and led her back to her own apartment.

'Charlie's milked the cows. You don't have to worry.' Marcia said to Mrs. Armitage.

'She should be in proper care,' Judith said, as she followed them.

'This doesn't happen all the time, she's all right really,' Marcia said.

Things seemed quiet for the next few days and then, one morning when Judith went out her front door to collect her newspaper, she nearly fell into a pile of rubbish in her porch. This was getting to be too much. Judith marched around to Mrs Armitage's french doors and found them open.

'Glenda,' she called as she stepped inside. 'Are you here?'

There was no answer. She ventured further in. There was no-one in the lounge or kitchen. She went down the hallway and heard water running in the bathroom. She tapped on the door and then opened it and there was Mrs. Armitage, standing half naked by her hand basin, her breasts hanging down to her waist like deflated balloons.

'I'm being burgled.' Mrs Armitage screamed. 'Help. Help.' She grabbed her stick and started hitting Judith on her head and shoulders.

'It's me, Judith, your neighbour,' Judith said as she tried to fend off the surprisingly strong Mrs. Armitage.

'Get out, get out,' Mrs Armitage screamed. I've had enough of you stealing my things.'

'I haven't stolen anything,' Judith said, as she held her arms up in front of her face.

Mrs. Armitage poked Judith in the stomach hard with her stick. Judith felt sick and winded. She pushed Mrs. Armitage away from her and then watched as she slowly toppled backwards into her bath. She lay there, blood from her head trickling down the white acrylic, legs up in the air, eyes staring horrified and unseeing at Judith.

'Oh my God,' Judith cried. She lifted Mrs. Armitage's hand and then let it go: it flopped on to Mrs. Armitage's stomach.

Judith stood there, frozen to the spot. This was a nightmare.

What should she do? Mrs. Armitage looked dead. Judith leaned down and felt the pulse in Mrs. Armitage's neck. No sign of life. She tried to calm herself. There was nothing anyone could do now and really, it was a good thing. Mrs. Armitage could be with Charlie and milk the cows for eternity. Here in the world, the woman was becoming a serious problem and it was obvious things would only get worse. After putting rubbish on her doorstep who knew what Mrs. Armitage would do next? No, this was a blessing in disguise, even for Mrs. Armitage. Judith just knew she had to look at it like that.

'I'm so sorry — Glenda,' Judith said, as she turned and quietly left, making sure no-one was watching as she slipped through the french doors.

She was just clearing the rubbish, amazed to see crumpled beer cans and fast-food wrappings amongst it, when Bob appeared.

'He's been at it again, has he?'

'Pardon?' She looked at him.

'Boozy Len. He gets paranoid when he gets on the grog and picks on someone he thinks is out to get him. This time it was your turn.'

'Oh.' Judith felt her mouth drop open. 'I thought…'

'You thought it was poor old Glenda?'

'Well, yes.'

'Nah, she wouldn't do a thing like that. She just gets a bit confused at times.' He looked at her. 'Are you coming to her party this afternoon?'

'Party?'

'Glenda's. It's her 95th birthday today. They're having a big "do" up at the facilities, her family will be here. There's been a notice about it in the restaurant. Everyone's invited.'

Judith stared at Bob. 'Goodness, I didn't realise Glenda was that old,' she managed to say.

'Got a good few years in her yet, I reckon,' Bob said.

'I'm sure she has,' Judith said, feeling as if her insides had dropped to her feet.

'So, will you come to her party? I know you've had trouble with her,' Bob said. 'But she's harmless really.'

Judith was desperate to say no, to say she felt ill, had another appointment, anything. And then she realised there wouldn't be a party. 'Of course I'll be there,' she said.

'There's always a bit of drama at Glenda's birthday,' Bob said. 'Last year she fell head first into her serving of pavlova and everyone thought she'd died. The year before, she slid down under the table and again, everyone thought she'd died. Who knows what'll happen this time?'

Judith tried to say something, but all she could feel was something like lava from a volcano rising up inside her. She couldn't stop it from coming. It rose higher and higher, burst out through her mouth and surged over Bob.

Oriental Bay – Rebecca Styles

Beryl can hear the cicadas' clicking, flickering, rattling hum from the hallway where she waits for Kember to collect her towel and togs. She has managed to get Kember away from Facebook-stalking a man she slept with a year ago; a man whose profile picture is a cartoon image of a banana with pins in it. Beryl had huffed at the image and tried not to think of a crude Freudian analysis. His profile also includes a picture of his 'real' self. Harry looks about ten years younger than Kember: he is blonde, Californian beach blond. Sleep lingers in the corner of his eyes and his slow insomnia-induced smile makes him look like a somnambulist. He works in visual media in Auckland. His profile page says, 'Harry projects images of physical and fantasy landscapes.' He doesn't go on-line or post messages as much as Kember would like. Beryl has watched Kember sit at the small square Formica table in the lounge with her laptop open refreshing the Facebook page every two minutes. She asked Beryl whether posting him messages every day and liking every comment he posts is too aggressive. Beryl said that she supposed so, that it would be best to lay off for a bit.

Beryl looks out the sash window. Cicadas live in the tree outside the flat. Kember said that the heat makes the insects sing, and that they live out their entire life-cycle on one tree. When they are young they start at the bottom of the tree then they move gradually up to the top to mate. The female cicadas then travel down the tree to lay eggs and so the cycle starts again.

Kember comes out of her room. She is underweight and revels in her fair-skinned and translucent lightness. She pulls up her singlet top and rubs what there is of her belly checking that her hip bones still jut out and pulls her top back down before asking Beryl if she's ready. Beryl has been ready for twenty minutes. Kember swings her

108

velvet patchwork bag coloured green, purple, and dirt over her shoulder, and makes her way downstairs. Beryl follows. Kember goes back into the house to fetch water, and then she stops at the dairy to get Panadol, and then she stops at the Freyberg pool to get a vegetable smoothie. As they stand on the footpath, waiting for the drink to be served, Beryl becomes aware, while surrounded by brightly clothed people, that she has chosen to wear a black t-shirt to the beach.

'This is better, I'm glad you suggested it. It's good to get away from worrying about Harry.'

Beryl returns Kember's comment with a thin-lipped smile.

Mid-afternoon at the bay. The sun brings out blisters of bodies on the beach; bodies in varying states of undress and modesty. Skin glistening with sweat. The sea is silenced under their weight. Flocks of families are huddled together — a large, festering, sunburnt mass. Parents' legs kick up sand as they scurry alongside the stick-like legs of their children whose feet frolic and run towards the water.

'How about we sit on the rocks in the shade, away from the families?'

Beryl nods and follows, wanting shelter for her emo complexion. She casts a look behind her and sees the children playing alongside the water's edge. A boy holds out a muscle shell he has dug up, shows it to another boy who snatches and holds onto it as if the green gills of the shell were as precious as greenstone, before dropping it into a small bucket.

The rocks are slabs of concrete. They have been piled up high and at varying angles as a child would assemble blocks on the living room floor to build a fort or perhaps a castle. They sit in a corner of the castle in a slither of shade that Beryl hogs while Kember clambers after the sun. The heat filters through Kember's sunscreen onto her ginger flecked skin and hair. Beryl hadn't really wanted to come to the beach but she thought she should make an attempt at friendship with Kember, rather than sit in her cool orderly bedroom and read the paper, which she only buys for the hope-laced horoscopes to banish the blues that call regularly on Sunday afternoons. Her Grandmother used to say that Sunday is a family day.

Down at the edge of the rocks there is a man, a bearded, jandaled, and shorts-wearing man who holds the hand of a girl, his child Beryl supposes, as they walk together. The man bends his back as he walks so he can hear his daughter who explains, while pointing at the water, what she can see beneath the surface. It's only when Beryl looks in the direction of the girl's pointed finger that she sees grass growing on the rocks. The man crouches right down beside the girl. They watch the grass waving under the water. The man turns away, he has been called. Beryl follows his line of sight to a woman. Beryl shuts her eyes. When she opens them she notices that a swell has swirled at the bottom of the slabs of concrete. She looks around to see if a boat has gone past, thinking that its wake has whipped up the sea, but she doesn't see a vessel. The swell appears to have come out of nowhere and then disappears leaving the lush green sea forest on the rocks swaying, a forest as thick and ragged as a buffalo's coat.

Kember wants to swim so they move from the slabs to a spare spot on the beach. Beryl notices that as she gets up the imprint of the castle rock has been etched onto her calf muscle. She rubs the dimpled surface of her leg and hopes that it will pop back to its usual firmness. She didn't realise that her skin was so malleable.

Kember drops her bag and walks towards the sea. She holds her hands out to her sides, level with the water, as if willing the waves to stay down, sit. Gradually she moves further in, deeper, up to the bottom of her khaki green board shorts, which Beryl thinks are very modest. With Kember's thinness and espousals that her friends ask her what it's like to be stick-thin and have all the men come after you because you've got the figure of a model, Beryl thought Kember would wear something more revealing. Kember braces herself and dives into the water and quickly comes back up. She wraps her arms around her chest and walks up the beach. Despite the heat Beryl notices Kember shiver as she walks towards her and the comfort of a towel.

'Oh my God I'm aching. It's soooo cold. Look at my skin.' Kember holds out her arm for Beryl's inspection. It looks like the blood has been wrung out of her system like the water seems to have washed the red out of her hair.

'Are you going to swim?'

'No. I didn't bring my togs.' Beryl sits on the beach, her legs stretched out in front of her, her arms behind her propping her up. She has lost her sunglasses so sits wearing her spectacles and squints in the sun. Her three quarter pants are too long, she feels too covered for the beach. The only thing bare is her feet. The water does look inviting but it's not quite how she imagines a beach should be. It is too crowded. It is too loud. It is not a beach where you can imagine that you're the only one who has walked on it today. The windows of the apartment blocks behind the bay glisten under the glare of the sun, and the panes seem to move as light and noise deflects from the traffic.

Beryl runs her hand through the rough sand: chips of scallop and pipi shells, a smooth piece of orange glass, stones, and shards of wood amongst the grain. Kember tells her that the sand was shipped in: black sand, Golden Bay sand, and cheap filler sand, deposited and packed onto the man-made beach. Beryl wonders if the whole beach is one of Harry's fantasy landscapes made physical, and the families are actors in the installation.

Kember, with her towel wrapped around herself, starts the awkward jiggle of someone trying to get out of her wet togs and back into her clothes without flashing the whole beach.

'These togs are too big. When I jumped up in the water my boob fell out, but only this little kid noticed. She pointed and looked at me with a look of horror.'

Beryl can't believe just how flat-chested Kember is and wonders whether the look of horror was for what the child saw, or for what the kid expected to see and didn't. Kember puts her t-shirt on and removes her bikini top out from underneath it. She rummages around in her bag.

'Oh God, I've forgotten my knickers.'

She discreetly dries between her legs, draws up her short denim skirt over the towel, zips the skirt up, and checks that the waist line doesn't ride too low on her hips.

Kember sits down on the beach, crosses her legs, and rolls a cigarette. She inserts the stubby filter at one end of the tissue paper and then places the tobacco inside, distributing it with her thumb and forefinger. She cups her other hand to protect the tobacco from the slight breeze and then rolls it together with her fingertips. Her touch is deft and the task seems domestic in its ordinariness. Beryl notices the tar stains on Kember's index finger and her ripped-up cuticles and torn skin. She has seen Kember use the serrated steak knife to rip and then smooth the cuticles and skin around her fingernails. She told Beryl that it releases endorphins, 'it's like self-harm' she said, 'rubbing my fingernails with my hand, or with the knife, releases a relaxing feeling, calms me down.' Beryl had wondered at the time if it was thinking about Harry that made Kember do it.

'You know, the thing about Harry is, I should just be his lover, one of many. It was better that way. I was a better person, fun, not such a muppet. This love stuff, it's just a fantasy.'

Kember doesn't look to Beryl for a response, instead she watches the children on the beach, drags on her cigarette, and attempts to puff smoke out of Beryl's way.

Kember stubs out her smoke on her water bottle and pops the butt into it, turns to Beryl and asks, 'How old are you?'

'26.'

'I'm 27. Do you want kids?'

'Um maybe, dunno.'

'Yeah, I'm a bit like that too. It's like I don't want to admit that I do want children otherwise there would be this constant longing, y'know.'

Beryl turns away, lies down on the towel on the fake sand and closes her eyes. It's only then that she hears the cicadas over the noise of the people and traffic, the insistent rattling hum.

The Snack Machine – Lawrence Patchett

We were headed for the park, me and Lucien. His mum was out for the morning and I was in charge again, for four hours this time. We were on track — he was breakfasted and dressed, ready for kicks, and I had the bag packed. We were set.

But now Lucien pulled out his mouthguard and eyed my bag.

'What?' I said.

Whatever it was, he would never answer a direct question like that.

I unzipped the bag. 'Here's your money pouch. It's all there. Kei te pai?'

He nodded, then faced the door again and waited. Each week after kicks we went to the gym that bordered the park so Lucien could buy a snack. There was a snack machine there; he used the pocket money he'd been given by his mum. It was serious, a tradition we'd set up — Lucien entrusted with his Mum's cash, me entrusted with him.

Now I eased the bag over my shoulders and tried not to wince — I'd had a bad back for some time, but it was getting better, and generally I tried to hide it from Lucien. This time he didn't seem to notice anyway. Out on the street he crunched along in his football boots. It was high summer, he didn't need boots, but he didn't need a mouthguard either. That was Lucien. Each week he got fully kitted out in his league gear — boots, headgear, Bears shirt — for a simple kickabout down the park. He was only seven. I could remember that kind of obsession, although cricket had been my thing when I was a kid.

The intersection came up and he waited for me.

'Ka pai,' I said. 'Safety first, eh?'

He nodded and looked for traffic.

We crossed and walked on in silence. The park was two blocks from our house, but sometimes it could seem quite a distance.

I gestured at the footpath ahead of us. 'Kei te haere tāua ki te *Paka Pea*,' I said, giving extra emphasis to *Paka Pea* to show that I meant it to be funny. I wasn't sure it equated to 'Bear Park', as I meant it to, but Lucien didn't seem to notice or consider it necessary to respond. Instead he watched his football boots, absorbed in their movements on the footpath.

'A great day for kicks,' I said. 'You might even be better in bare feet, mate. You could get blisters in boots. The ground's hard at this time of year.'

He looked up at me with his headgear framing his serious face, then at his boots. No comment.

'Ah well,' I said. 'He ātaahua tēnei rā!'

A bit more walking, no traffic, the silence pressing down. Lucien's mother assured me that the boy liked me; he was just reserved, still getting to know me. And I knew that he didn't think much of my reo, even though it was for his sake that I was learning — mostly for his sake. It was something about me that he tolerated, at best.

We made the car park, then the park itself. I handed him the ball and lifted the chain fence so he could scramble under. Slowly with the ball in his arms he walked out into the park, his boots not sinking into the hard turf. As for me I laid the bag carefully, then ran onto the open grass, briefly elated in the sunshine and space, my back and shoulders much better than last time.

Then I turned to see Lucien standing about five paces into the field with the ball held rigid in front of him. He was lining up his first kick. Solemnly he stared at the ball, gauged and re-gauged it. I couldn't watch. So much concentration; I felt the tension of it in my own back.

'Kia kaha, mate!' I shouted. 'Boot it!'

For another aching moment the ball was poised in front of him, too high up, too far out. Then he threw it up high and lurched out with his leg. It was an inelegant karate chop, rather than a fluid kick, but it was a connection at least, and the ball came a fair way towards me, far enough to celebrate.

'Awesome!' I said. 'Well done!'

He adjusted his headgear and waited. With my left foot I chipped it back. On the bounce it went over his head and he ran after it, zigzag, still too inexperienced to anticipate the bounce. Then the procedure was repeated, Lucien's face tight with concentration, his tongue-tip stuck out while he readied the kick. This time the ball struck the end of his boot and it hurt him — I could see it immediately, that snapping foot-shock you get when you don't strike it right. Not that he would show it.

I rushed him a thumbs up. 'Good man!'

With his sore foot held out to the side, he watched me, lopsided.

After a few kicks I shortened the distance between us, because he never kicked as well once he'd hurt his foot, and because I could spiral-pass it back, which helped to ease my shoulders, whereas standing in anxious wait for his kicks tended to do the opposite.

Now he was lining up a drop kick, arms clamping the ball way out in front. He stowed the ball and fished his mouthguard out. 'Davy? Can I tackle you?'

'Absolutely,' I said. 'Bring it.'

He replaced the mouthguard and sent his kick up. On the bounce it came within easy reach and I curled round it, bracing for the hit. As he came closer I wailed in pretend panic.

Just before impact Lucien laughed, ecstatic at my dramatics and the excitement of it, and as we mauled and growled and wrestled for the ball, I laughed too, relieved to have made a breakthrough. It was often this way with him, the rough and tumble achieving what other kinds of play couldn't. We repeated the kick and tackle procedure, each maul more boisterous than the last, circling in the centre of the field in our loose rumble.

Then he tackled me again and I fell down in exaggerated fashion, as if felled by a mighty hit, but this time on impact I hit the ground differently and shrieked for real. I'd hit the ground badly, twisted my neck, made it all worse. Pain gripped my whole back.

Lucien was above me. 'Are you all right?'

'Absolutely,' I said. 'Taihoa, mate. I'll be up in a sec.'

My back was frozen all the way up, the pain most acute right between my shoulder blades. Lying on the ground I saw another month of bad sleeps and chiropractor visits ahead, and for once I had a good swear about it.

Lucien stiffened. He wasn't allowed to use bad language himself.

'Go back and have another kick, mate,' I said. 'It's all right — go back. I'm just going to lie here for a minute.'

'Kay.'

I lay still a moment longer, then pushed up on my left arm, crying out at the spike of pain this sent into my shoulders.

Ten metres away, Lucien watched as I stood, crookedly. 'Have you hurt your back?' he said.

No shit, I wanted to say, and didn't.

I signalled him to send up another one, and when it came I caught the ball and lobbed it back to him, so he could do the running now. He tore away and giggled across the grass, the ball huge in his arms.

'Rah!' I said, in very slow and sore-backed pursuit. 'Bears!'

I'd shown him how to sidestep, and he used it on me now, nipping left just as I got there, chortling with excitement. I couldn't keep it up.

I pointed at the goalposts. 'Place kicks?'

Taking out his kicking tee I spun it towards him, then went to the goalposts, took my books out and lay with my feet propped on the bag. This had become a tradition too. Each week when my back got too sore I lay with my legs on my bag to form a sort of second crossbar. If Lucien kicked the ball over the real crossbar he got three points; over my legs was two points. He seldom got either — mostly the ball squirted along the ground or struck my head or hands as I read my book — but it was a good custom. He enjoyed it.

I settled crankily down and took out my reo practice-books.

Turning through cartoons of kuri and ngeru, of smiling tamariki, I felt a momentary slump of enthusiasm. It took me so long to learn so little. And Lucien didn't respond to it — and for some reason his mum had stopped using her own reo round the house. Perhaps my learning embarrassed her somehow, my eagerness making her wince for my sake. All the same I had a test coming, so I went through the cartoons again, pencilling in the crossword answers in the speech-bubbles. *He aha tēnei? He kuri tēnā! He aha tērā? He whare tērā!* I was getting through the exercises when I sensed Lucien coming. I twisted up to see him, and he stopped, suddenly abashed, still a few metres back.

'What's up?' I said. 'It's all right. Just tell me what it is.'

'What's the time, Davy?'

'Twelve-thirty.'

He looked across the park to the gym. 'I'll stop my kicks at twelve-fifty to get my snack.'

'Okay.'

'Because if I leave it till one o'clock it might be too late.'

'You can take longer if you want to,' I said. 'It won't matter if we're a few minutes late.'

'But Mum said to get back at one-fifteen, cause we're going to Dad's after that.'

'Good point,' I said. 'So at twelve-fifty I'll stop you and we'll go across to get your snack. Enjoy your kicks now, mate.'

'Kay.' He put his mouthguard back in and went back.

I watched the first kick and shouted some encouragement because he got some air on it, and said he could come closer to the goalposts if he wanted, to which he shook his head. Then I went back to my workbooks, where two cartoon children were walking through a village. A motokā went past them; an awa passed under a bridge. I followed them all the way to the shops, and pencilled in their comments. I checked on Lucien and leaned back with eyes closed. He had given up the place kicks and was chipping the ball and running after it, absorbed in his own experiments. I left him to it,

117

closed my eyes again and took a few minutes for myself. I thought of my girlfriend. She was in Porirua this morning, squeezing in two catch-ups with mates. A good break for her from Lucien. The sun was high now. I closed my eyes and enjoyed the heat, too sore to relax right away, but pleasantly lethargic.

I woke with a start. Lucien was right above me. At that angle his face had a contorted look, and I flashed with the worst-case panic of step-parenting — a dog had bitten him, he was bleeding from some hidden wound; his appendix had burst and was flooding him with poison.

'Are you hurt?' I said. 'What is it, Lucien?'

'What's the time, Davy?'

I shot a look at my watch. 'Let's go,' I said. 'Did you enjoy your place kicks?'

I felt his eyes on me as I scrambled to shove books, kicking tee, drink bottle in the bag. We were late and he knew it. He marched straight out into the park, short legs walking fast, not toeing the ball ahead as he sometimes did. Stiff-backed, I lurched along behind in low-grade panic. We were only fifteen minutes late, at this point. It wouldn't matter. His mum wouldn't mind. But it was a long way across the park, and hot, and I was sweating by the time we made the small hill before the gym.

In the foyer, no one was at the snack machine. Lucien went straight across to it. I tried not to watch as he stood on tiptoes to examine the snacks and feed his coins. I scanned the empty foyer, the few gymsters who were coming and going, red-faced from exercise. I wondered idly at the kupu for snack machine. Te mīhini kai, perhaps. I'd ask my girlfriend later. She had more reo than me. She had the background.

Lucien was back.

'Problem?' I said. 'Can't you decide?'

He didn't want to say.

'Come on, Lucien,' I said. 'We're running a bit late; your mum—'

'The machine took all my fifty centses and my dollar, and it won't give me anything back.'

I stood up. 'Come and we'll sort this out.'

At the machine he showed me the button he'd pushed, the empty refund slot. His eyes were huge. 'There's nothing,' he said.

I took over then. I fished coins from my own pocket and slotted them, pushed the buttons and waited. Lucien was silent and small beside me, looking up. It didn't work. I tried again with more coins and lost them too. Reaching down to the refund slot a stab of pain went between my shoulders, there were no coins, and I flared with a sudden immoderate rage.

'Fuck's sake!' I said, slamming the refund button with my thumb. 'Scheisse! Stupid … fricking … scheissing … what? Pardon?'

Lucien had mumbled something, but now that I'd whirled on him he shrank back and couldn't repeat it.

'Lucien — what?' I said. 'Come on, we haven't got all day here.'

'Don't say Māori all the time.'

'What?'

'Don't talk Māori all the time. It's annoying.'

'That wasn't even Māori. I said scheisse. That's German. It's not even—' I breathed deep, closed my eyes. I was getting overheated; I'd hurt my thumb by jabbing the buttons, to go with my sore shoulders and back. 'Never mind. It's okay, Lucien. I'm going to fix this problem here. I'll go get the lady. You stay here, all right?'

He wouldn't look me in the face.

'I'm sorry,' I said. 'My back's hurting me, but that's not your fault. Sorry I swore. Just wait here, Lucien. We can fix this.'

No response.

I put my hand on his shoulder. 'It's all right. I'll get the lady for us.'

There was no one at the desk. I hit the bell and peered into the staff-only area, hit the bell again. At last a guy shambled out. I tried not to flare at his casual approach.

'I'm sorry to drag you out,' I said. 'Lucien here — his pocket money. The machine swallowed it and gave him nothing back.'

119

The guy sighed and shook his head at the machine as if our complaint was not a new one. 'Yeah, it's poked — it's been poked for ages.'

'Could you fix it, please,' I said, my voice tightening.

He looked at my face, then ambled back towards the staffroom. 'Back in a minute,' he said.

I went back to Lucien. 'We'll have it fixed in a sec.'

'Kay,' said Lucien. He was now absorbed in watching a game of basketball in the main gym, his eyes tracing the ball left and right.

The guy came back with a special key. It was a T-shaped thing and it fitted into a slot under the bottom of the door. He swung the whole glass frontage away to expose the snacks. For a moment Lucien and I just stared at them, the snacks all lined up on their spiral displays, somehow smaller without the glass in front, their magic gone away.

Lucien watched as the guy thumbed a button to empty the metal deposit box of its coins.

'How much did you put in?' he said.

Lucien half-looked at me, then said, 'Two dollars fifty. Please.'

'That's right,' I said. 'Good man, Luce.'

The guy counted out Lucien's coins, then swung the glass door shut. Lucien reached his coins in again, punched the buttons, waited. Again it didn't work; again he looked at me, big-eyed.

'Oh shittin' hell,' said the guy. 'The machine's poked.'

'Maybe you could just hand Lucien's chips to him?' I said. 'It might be easier. Sorry.'

'God, don't apologise, mate,' he said. 'It's not your fault. The machine's poked — it's been poked for ages. I rang the service company, but they just—'

'Could you just grab some chips for Lucien?' I said. 'We haven't got much time.'

'Sure,' he said, catching my tone properly this time. With his key he unlocked the front again and brought forth two bags for Lucien, shoving them right into Lucien's hands. Surprised, the boy stared at this sudden solution.

'Look at that!' I said. 'That's nice, eh?'

He nodded, too shy to say anything.

'Lucien, was that what you wanted?' I said. 'Kei te pai?'

'Yep.'

'Excellent — look, thanks so much,' I said, to the guy. 'You're a lifesaver.'

'Not a problem,' he said, swinging the door shut.

'No, you've got no idea,' I said. 'You've saved me an opera, here. This could have been a *big* tragedy, for us.'

He laughed and something unpleasant passed between us as we both recognised my sudden disloyalty to Lucien. But the boy was watching the basketball again, fixated.

'All right,' I said. 'Thanks again.' I took Lucien by the shoulder and guided him out.

On the hill leading down to the sports field it was bright, and Lucien lifted up to me his new bags of chips. I was to keep them in my bag, he said.

'Don't you want to eat them now?' I said. 'You can if you want.'

'I'll save them,' he said.

Normally he ate them on the way back, but not today, apparently. Whatever. I stowed them and worked the bag over my shoulders, still very cramped.

Lucien looked up. 'Can we do kick and chase?'

I looked across the park and sighed. In five minutes I'd be home and his mum would be back, and I'd get a break, an hour or two out the back with my bikes. A coffee maybe — and painkillers. I pictured the exact place of the painkillers in the kitchen cupboard, saw myself taking them from the shelf and cracking the seal. 'Sure,' I said. 'I can't chase today, though. I'll kick and you chase.'

He agreed to this. I sent out a contorted punt and he ran straight after it, then zigzagged, tracking it. Watching him go, I smiled. He was using up his energy, all right. He'd be knackered after this; he'd fall mute before a DVD or his books, and his mum would thank me for it. Then I remembered he was going to his dad's, straight after, and we were late. Whatever. We wouldn't be more than half an hour late, maybe 45 minutes. Besides, it was good to get him active. No one could complain about that.

My second kick came off the side of my shoe, and with my third I made the car park, Lucien running towards the chains, then checking for traffic before going into the car park to scoop it up.

'Hang onto it now,' I said, calling ahead. 'Watch for cars, please.'

He waited for me, still getting his breath back. Together we crossed the car park and made for the footpath, Lucien puffed and carrying the ball. Moisture had darkened his headgear where it met his neck. He'd worked up a sweat. What a good kid, I thought.

We walked on a bit and I saw our car up ahead. My girlfriend was back from Porirua — Lucien hadn't seen it yet. He was trundling along beside me in his boots, listening to their crunching on the asphalt.

'Salt and vinegar's not my favourite,' he said, suddenly.

'What?' I said.

'Salt and vinegar — that man gave me salt and vinegar chips. They're not my favourite.'

'Really?' I said. 'What flavour did you select?'

'Original.'

'Yeah, I like original too,' I said. 'But salt and vinegar's not too bad.'

He studied his boots as he thought about this. 'I don't *not* like it,' he said. 'It's just not my favourite.'

I laughed. 'That's right.'

'Mum's back,' he said, and ran ahead.

I lunged to grab his shoulder, to pull him back. He'd run straight into the intersection, almost.

'Wait please, Lucien,' I said. 'Remember? Taihoa, then tītiro, then hikoi.'

He stood very still and sighed, looked in all four directions, then walked with exaggerated slowness beside me to the other side —

then ran ahead again, plunging through our gate and front door and into the kitchen. Inside I heard him shout, heard his mother exclaiming over him. She was happy to see him, I could hear it. The break had refreshed her.

I was still on the footpath outside. Gingerly I removed my bag and massaged my neck. It was thoroughly cramped again, and my shirt was damp with sweat. Up ahead the street was clear of traffic, the sun pounding down bright and unrestrained on the asphalt. Behind me the car contracted and clicked, still hot from the trip to Porirua and back. I pushed through our gate and went in. Lucien's arms were round her neck. Peering past his headgear she smiled at me. I removed my bag and smiled back.

Green Man – Kay Meyer

Perhaps I do tend to take things personally. That may be what my ex-wife Mara meant when she said once I was the most self-referring person she'd ever met. I must have looked blank because she added, 'When someone tells you about the mote in his eye, you can't wait to tell him about the beam in yours,' which left me not much wiser. I do worry about my health but my eyes have never given me any problem.

As it happens, I was in the doctor's waiting room when I read the newspaper article. *Marriage Saves Planet* shouted the headline. My interest was piqued. I wanted to find out whose marriage had performed this miracle. You can imagine how disappointed I was, disappointed and affronted by the next words: 'Staying married is better for the planet because divorce leads the newly single to live more wasteful—' and the rest of the article had been ripped away by another patient salvaging something, probably a coupon.

I was at that time quite recently divorced but I was surprised to find how indignant I felt, and continued to feel about the article. After all it isn't generally divorcees who choke the nation's landfills with disposable nappies. There was no follow-up news story, so I resorted to the internet to find out what shonky piece of research had been behind the article. I couldn't find anything further there either.

But I did find another story, one about a couple who, by recycling diligently, managed to use only one Council rubbish sack every six months. I'll show them, I thought — the them being those anonymous researchers, not the green couple — a divorced man can be just as kind to the environment. Being my usual rational self for a moment, I back-pedalled to a goal of one Council sack every six weeks. And of course I would need a compost heap. The net provided a lot of good advice about getting one going. I'm not the

DIY type, so I bought a black plastic bin from the garden centre.

There was one issue: I live on the upper-floor of a two-storied block of flats. I share a carport in the front and a yard under weedy pavers at one side with the woman in the flat below. There's no garden, a feature which appealed to me when I first saw the place. The foot of the stairs leading to my front door, and my neighbour's flower pots, pretty much fill the yard, but there was room for the compost bin in the corner. I hadn't seen much of the neighbour since I'd come to live there. As she was obviously a gardener of sorts, I supposed she'd be sympathetic to my green endeavours.

Storage of the Council rubbish sack while it was filling posed more of a difficulty. In the end I put it in a carton at the back of the carport.

Around that time, I began to feel I should be re-joining the human race, or more particularly, the other half of it. I'm a consulting accountant — a financial hygienist, I like to say — brought in by desperate corporates to clean up their accounting systems. I meet most people rather fleetingly and spend much of my day alone with a computer. After twelve years of marriage I feared that the mechanics of courtship might have seized up in me.

You may be surprised to learn that playing away from home was not a factor in my divorce — and Mara knew it. I overheard her telling a friend on the phone, 'Of course I'm sure. Adam's too self-involved to have an affair with anyone else.'

Anyway, I needed to test-run my conversational skills. My car had been a casualty of the divorce, so evenings usually found me on a crowded central city bus-stop. For some days I'd been nodding and smiling at a small woman in a big coat and one of those woolly hats with the braids hanging down beside the cheeks. I tried a few inconsequential remarks. Though her responses were monosyllabic, her smile was benign, if a bit distant. Suddenly she blurted, 'I'm sorry, I missed what you just said. I was thinking about my worm farm.'

I was a bit startled. I tried not to take the remark personally. Surely I hadn't so completely forgotten the craft of small talk? I still had my mouth ajar when the woman climbed on a bus and was gone.

It was later that same week that I found a terse letter from the Council's public health department requesting my presence at home the following Saturday morning. In person the inspector, Gregory Somerville, turned out to be the mild-mannered sort. There'd been a complaint from Mrs van der Wilt at 2A about a smelly rubbish sack in the carport. She wasn't happy about the compost bin either. My neighbour, her face like a congested strawberry, was breathing heavily down the inspector's neck.

I explained about my recycling ideas. Mrs van der Wilt looked at me as if I were barking. One corner of Somerville's mouth twitched upwards. I apologised for the sack and promised to abandon that part of my experiment.

'Why didn't you just tell me it was a problem instead of bothering the Council?' I asked Mrs van der W, hoping to wrong-foot her and gain favour with the inspector at the same time. 'I'm sure Gregory — er, Mr Somerville here, must have more serious public health threats to deal with.'

My neighbour was not to be deterred. 'What about the stinky bin?'

We were standing in the yard by this time. I, quoting from the internet primmer on composting, 'A well maintained compost bin does not have an unpleasant odour.' I crossed my fingers behind my back. I'll acknowledge it: I don't have a good sense of smell.

Somerville sniffed. He temporised. 'Well, I have to say … there's only the *slightest* whiff of vegetal decay and it's not illegal to have a compost bin, you know. On the other hand, it's still only early spring and in summer there could be an issue…'

'…with flies and vermin.' Mrs van der Wilt's tone was righteous.

'The compost's covered. You don't see any flies, do you? And with your cat around all the time,' I gestured at the large orange beast sunning himself on the lid, 'there won't be any problem with rats or mice either. Just think, you won't have to buy any fertiliser for your tulips.'

She protested the cat wasn't hers, but I'd scored a point with my lucky guess about the tulips. To a background of Somerville's helpful murmurs Mrs van der Wilt agreed the bin could stay — for the time being.

I'm indifferent to pets in general but the cat, frankly, made me uneasy: The scar, which started at the corner of his mouth and disappeared into the thick fur of his cheek, gave him a cynical air. It was only when I was watching a documentary about the 70s that I realised who he resembled. How Muldoon ended up sitting beside me on the couch in front of the television after a fruitless month spent looking for his owner, is another story.

It was a mistake to tell Mara about the run-in with my neighbour. 'Being able to grow mushrooms in your dirty socks does not make you green, Adam,' she said. A remark I considered both inaccurate and unfair: I'm fussy about personal hygiene.

The woman at the bus stop was more sympathetic. By this time we'd exchanged names. Hers was Tui Greenwood and she worked for the Department of Conservation. 'My parents are life members of Forest and Bird,' she said. 'Thank you for not laughing.'

I didn't tell her Mara says I have no sense of humour. It seemed safer just to observe that parents have a lot to answer for.

Tui, without her winter coat and pixy hat, was younger and more attractive than I'd thought. She was also a great source of advice about my worm farm.

I suppose you think I should have learned something from my recycling experiments (you're a slow learner, Adam, I can hear Mara saying) but I really didn't expect any problem with setting up a little farm on the deck at the top of my stairs. There wasn't much room but I didn't, as Mrs van der Wilt alleges, put it right over her front door intentionally.

Of course I understand she wasn't happy about being spattered with worm wee as she set out in her bowling whites one Saturday morning. I don't know how the collection tray could have slipped out of place. I wondered if Muldoon had upset it. He was certainly strong enough: I'd caught him jemmying the door of my old fridge with his paw. Mrs van der Wilt berated me for trying to shift the blame on to the poor, dear cat. It took payment of her dry cleaning bill, two bottles of wine and Gregory's good offices to mollify her. I also had to promise to get rid of the worms.

Tui put her briefcase down on the pavement and laughed herself to hiccups when I told her the story. I didn't mind. But I found I did mind that she might somehow discover what a sickly shade of green I really was, so I confessed I didn't have a garden. To my astonishment she said she didn't either. She was renting one up the Valley from an old woman who couldn't manage it any more. 'Prime market garden land and she was going to put it under concrete. Can you imagine!' I didn't say that, until I met her, this response to an unwanted garden would have seemed to me quite reasonable.

Our buses came and went without us. 'You know,' Tui said, 'I think it would be a good idea if your worms came to live with mine.'

Not the most alluring proposition. But I've learned not to take such things personally.

Flower, Flowers – Wendy Moore

Once every year, when one of us opens the front door of our fourth-floor flat in Ružinov, there is a pink gerbera. A single flower, unlabelled, could be for either or both of us. It is neither the same pink year on year, nor the same pink as over a decade ago.

In her calm way, my wife, Beata, makes no fuss. 'You must have an admirer,' she says.

'Or you,' I reply every year, also calmly. Only occasionally do I feel overwhelmed by what my stupidity wrought. I hope after all these years that the danger has passed. The Mafia profile is vastly reduced and their focus now on skimming EU contracts.

In the late winter of twelve years ago, the Danube sneaked extremely high. The low-lying island of Ostrov Sihot' was spread entirely with water. The main river behind became foreground also. Steadily and dangerously it rolled grey-green and hell bent on reaching the Black Sea, but without the appearance of rushing too much.

My then partner, Elise, didn't rush anywhere and her preoccupation with her health made living with her hell.

'My back's gone — it's all the books,' she'd say with satisfaction as she hooked on her overfull backpack. She would head out the door to school, gloom-laden. 'Can't get down on the floor with the kids. Knees have seized up.'

We all felt Seasonal Affective Disorder to varying degrees, but Elise's was the most deeply suffered. Like that particular Saturday, when I was trying to cajole her out of the flat.

'Come on, darling, we need to do the shopping.'

'I don't want to get out of bed, Dan,' she whined. 'I'm just so miserable. I…'

I wished that I could leave Elise behind and get on with my life. I switched off and exited the flat — lift out of order, down four flights — into the cold-burning wind. It was recognisably winter even without the sight of the flooded river: grey skies clamped firmly in place with industrial smog.

The next passing tram had taken me down to the Danube, then a bus along to the ruined castle. There, the long grass slurped and moaned, flattened, but mostly released from its snow cover. Silver birches earned their name as the ice-smeared trunks twinkled and the bare branches whispered as they scraped in the wind. In the tepid sunlight the ice on the trunks would suddenly snap, as gunshot, and fall in curved shards.

I felt so alone in the world. Alone and drowning, drowning in Elise and her neediness. Maybe a cigarette? One of my infrequent ones. I reached into my pocket: two cigarettes, no matches.

The castle seemed built for a gothic movie. The ice-scalloped edges of the wooden steps, safe when snow-covered, were dangerous and I moved cautiously. Exquisite blue ice was exposed as the day warmed; the trip down could be quick indeed.

But I was not alone. At the top, a woman. Sheltering from the wind, pitting her cigarette lighter against it. Could I have a light, I asked?

'Sure, Anglo,' holding out her lighted cigarette.

I drew mine from it. 'I wasn't expecting you to speak English.'

'Why not? I lived for five years in the UK.' Then, holding out her hand, she introduced herself. 'Kvetoslava.'

It is not long before I love Kvetoslava, and do so even after I discover her dark secrets. Life becomes a jigsaw of meeting up.

'Don't phone me, don't text me,' she says.

But of course. She is married to a Slovak she met in London. However, *she* texts *me* and we have coffee, never openly. She works only a little. 'My husband wants to support me.'

She dislikes her excessive smoking as much as I. When we are together, I try to get her to cut down.

She shrugs, resignedly. 'I put on a few kilos when I first came back but I've lost it again,' she tells me. She is slender, not overly thin. The generous breasts, the minimalist hips, the long legs, the quintessential Slav of this part. And the hair neither blonde nor corn, just gold-yellow in the light.

We take to having coffee and a drink together at the flat of her friend, who owns the nearby florist shop where Kvetka works. It is convenient for me too, quite near the newspaper office. My knowledge of the language is my biggest asset here: learned as a child from my émigrée grandmother during long, hot, New Zealand summers together. With the freedom of a freelancer plus some translation, I am my own man.

It is a long time before we go to bed together. Another winter, less harsh, is nearly gone before it happens. One heavy snowfall: otherwise, tiny cotton-drifts of snow that go nowhere, except back into the ether. Elise has also gone, left the country. She writes that her back feels much better after six months in Spain, though often the heat is all but unbearable to her.

Kvetka's and my love has been like cotton-drift also, until now. We curl up on the large couch, my arm round her shoulders. She burrows into me, with a desire for safe haven. But any neediness is that of talk, she doesn't wish or want prompting. Often there are long gaps.

'You know why I smoke so much, Dan-ee-el?' she asks.

After a pause, I nod for her to continue.

'Ivan says that he will throw me out if I put on weight.'

I cannot say, 'Weight? What does weight matter? Leave him and come and live with me.'

One time later, she has a bruise on her forehead. I only know because, as we are drifting in peaceful silence, I stroke her hair.

She winces. 'I was tired. I didn't want to go out drinking with him and his friends.'

I can only hold her close, and so we drift.

Then she arrives one day and I cannot help but notice the diamond bracelet on her wrist. This is the real McCoy. We talk. I ignore. We talk. She ignores. It is only after an hour, and two coffees, when she is curled into my shoulder, that I reach out. There is no playing with such a heavy-duty piece of jewellery. It is firm to the wrist and as I turn it once — not easily — I see there is no clasp.

I take that hand in mine. 'Did it hurt?' I stupidly ask, and she shrugs. But maybe we are less drifting.

It is one afternoon, soon after that, when we first make love. Purposefully, she takes my hand and leads me over to the bed. She first grips my shoulders to show that I must not assist while she takes off my clothes, then drops to her knees and lifts her mouth. And then she is on her back as we slip into each other and my life is transported upwards, into the stratosphere.

And thus, in the following months, we are no longer drifting. I can give her the warmth and comfort of soft-solid love. She gives me sexual-soul closeness, a satisfaction never felt before. We meet more often, we breathe each other deeply.

I try saying to myself, 'Take care, take care. Beware, beware.'

We meet sometimes by coincidence. Once she comes into the office while I am there and she acknowledges me with her eyes.

'I want to advertise a flat to rent,' she says to the receptionist, who knows that her husband, Ivan, owns many flats.

Sometimes I see her — hoping to — as I swing by the florist's shop and she makes her lips curve up at the flowers she is holding, without looking at me.

This particular time I enter the shop. It is the name day of an office colleague. It's also a hot day and I say I'll pick up the flowers later.

In the shop doorway, I reach forward to give Kvetka a touch of farewell. I do not see, nor hear, anything, but through the slight intake of breath through her nostrils, sense a change. She bends down: it is a blindingly pink gerbera she uplifts from the container.

'Twenty korun.' The flower held out in one hand, the other hand outstretched and cupped. A slight shift of her eyes.

I fumble for a coin, drop it into her hand. Only then do I follow the focus of her eyes; like her, not moving my head.

Black car, shaded windows. Only a concentration of will stops me reacting and makes me able to smile, nod, turn, and walk away. There is blood taste in my mouth and I throw the flower in a bin near the office.

The next night there is a phone call.

'Kveta is here.' the voice says. 'Come to this address.'

I go where it has told me. Ivan is there, and he pumps my hand up and down — his fleshy, but toned.

'I know that you would want to see Kveta one last time,' he says.

An impassive funeral director leads me to the open coffin in the next room.

She is, if possible, more beautiful. Her make-up, sometimes too strong, is soft and subtle. The faint green on her eyelids would reflect hazel eyes, were they open. The perfect arch of the brows. I feel ill and dizzy: these details I can see, but hardly see. The pink gerbera, tucked behind one ear and partly clouded by the rippling gold, consumes my vision. I want to stroke her hair in an effort to bring her back to life.

As I curl a tendril behind the ear, the pink flower shifts and I see make-up covering a jagged, mended hole. With the next stroke of the yellow-gold, the flower is repositioned by my thumb. Have I seen what I have seen?

And has Ivan seen my movement? When I look up, he is standing opposite me. Moving to the foot of the coffin he holds out his hand;

I propel myself towards it. Does he wink as we shake?

With an almost imperceptible movement of the head, the funeral director shows me the way. Still without a word, he opens a door and I am out on the street.

I lingered. I remained. I married Beata. We have children. I am happy with my life now — except for the annual reminder of the gerberas.

(Kvetoslava is a Slovak name from kvet, 'a flower.' Kveta is a pet name from it; Kvetka an even more affectionate shortening.)

No Going Back – Janet Nixon

She came in out of the cold, pain written all over her face, her eyes red and swollen. Her mascara had escaped its usually flawless lines, staining her cheeks.

Oh God it's happened. I only had to look at her.

She nodded and moved towards me. I held her tight as she sobbed. It sounded as if each sob was shredding her from the inside out.

'It's over,' she said.

Was it only three months ago that the sun had come out for her? We'd met for our regular coffee, as we'd done for 20 years, ever since our small children thrust us upon each other. I hadn't seen her for a few weeks. She had arrived late, breathless, flushed, her eyes shining like she was on some designer drug.

She'd met someone. This one was different.

Yeah right, I thought. Her track record was like a discarded TAB betting slip. She'd put money on so many sure-fire winners, so many men that had never crossed the finish line. A solitary old age would have been a more certain thing to put a dollar or two on.

We sat at an outside table in the late summer sun, the kind of sun that warms your bones. It imprints its heat on your DNA, making a deposit to carry you through winter.

We ordered coffee.

'Do you want something to eat?' I offered.

'No thanks. I've lost interest in food.'

I got her a brownie anyway. 'Are you sleeping?'

'No. I just lie there thinking about him all night.'

Okay. She's got it bad.

The coffee arrived.

'Are you sure this is decaf?' I asked the waitress. I didn't want to lose any sleep.

I knew what the conversation was going to be about. 'Tell me.'

'He's gorgeous, intelligent, funny, and he sails. He lives in Miramar and works in the film industry.'

'Single? Divorced? Kids?' I queried. They don't usually come unfettered at our age.

She paused, her radiance ebbing away. 'Ummm … yeah, two kids, and, ah … married.'

Oh shit. I didn't say anything. I couldn't. I'd had my own sailor, slightly different scenario. I'd been the married one, and with the child. I'd left the husband devastated, left my old life looking like the aftermath of a tsunami.

What she said next was straight from Mills and Boon. I could have been completely cynical about it, but I knew it was possible.

'He says the relationship is over. It's not working. He was on his way out when we met.'

His wife had had an affair. The relationship hadn't been the same since, so the story went. I wanted to say 'yeah right,' but years ago I'd told a similar story myself.

She knew her ethics were suspect. That she should wait till he'd left his wife. She was a family court mediator in the justice system for God's sake. But she didn't wait.

I ate the brownie.

I'd met him many times since then. He was gorgeous, a silver haired version of Harrison Ford. They'd visit and drink a couple of glasses of wine. They'd sit at my table, almost inhaling each other. He couldn't keep his hands off her. It was like I was invisible. They never stayed long, just apologetically slunk away to her flat. The traces of their hunger echoed long after the lovers' departure.

Last time we'd met, the leaves on the tree outside the café had turned red and gold, drifting down to join their friends on the pavement. Our tans had faded. We'd moved inside by the fire. That day she had dark circles under her eyes. She'd even ordered the brownie, and eaten it. I waited.

'There was an accident. His son, the 15-year-old, was in a car with some older teenagers. Drunk. They ran a stop sign, wiped out another car. He went through the windscreen. It's touch and go.'

We sat.

'I know I should let him go, let him be with his family. I feel such a bitch, but I can't.'

Last week she'd told me he had been all set to leave his wife at the end of the month. He'd planned it all out, the house, the money, the settlement. He was moving out and moving in with her. They were already building dreams and goals together. The prospect of old age being a solitary time was gone. Life wasn't going to be 'working till she was 65', retiring, and taking up crochet. She had a future, a purpose, and someone to share it with.

'Tell me why you think you should let him go,' I asked.

'So many reasons,' she said. 'They are screaming around in my head, making me feel like crap. That kid doesn't need some other woman shredding his parent's marriage right now. His father needs to focus on the boy and the family, not on me. And it could be a long haul.'

'And…?'

'I guess it could bring him closer to his wife,' she finally said.

'How do you know he doesn't need you more than ever right now?'

'Yeah I know, but she needs him, and she's the mother. Why does it all have to be so hard?'

On that early winter's day when she'd come to my house in tears, the season's first icy winds had wrenched the last of the leaves off the trees. She told me she'd gone to the funeral, sat at the back swaddled in a big black scarf. There they were, holding hands, arms around each other. She knew. This was not the time. It may never be the time. She grieved too, not about the boy, but about the loss of hope, the dissolving of what was going to be.

She'd gone home and sent him an email.

The trees were budding, it was still a little chilly but we could sit outside again.

'So what's new?'

'I've met someone…'

Grandad's Shadow – Margaret Orange

'Mum, do I have to?' Two nights and two days! It's forever, thought Philip. 'I might be getting a bug, Mum. Lots of kids have to stay home from school cos they've got a bug.'

His mother smiled. 'Don't be silly, Phil.' She closed the window and pulled the curtains. 'You'll be fine,' she said. 'Nan could do with some company. Anyway we'll be back on Sunday around four. Now, everything that you'll need is on your bed. Pack, please, and take some books and a puzzle. You might run out of things to do.'

While he stuffed his gear into the bag and humped it into the hall Mum hurried to the kitchen.

'Good lad, we'll be on our way as soon as Dad gets home. You'll have a great time. I'm sure Nan's looking forward to having you, you know.'

Before Grandad died it had always been fun to stay over, but last summer, before he had his sixth birthday, was the very best time. They did things together. Pottering, Grandad called it, in the garden and the tool shed.

'We'll get out of your way, Jane,' he'd say to Nan. 'We've got pottering to do, haven't we, old chap?' and before you knew it lunch was ready or Grandad would say, 'The sun's on its way to England, it'll be dark soon, Phil,' and it was time to go indoors.

Phillip liked it when Grandad called him 'old chap'; it gave him a best mate feeling, and when Nan said 'young man' he felt almost grown-up. She made the yummiest dinners. Her kitchen smelled chocolaty-biscuity and she spoiled him with mugs of tea. He was allowed two teaspoons of sugar, too. That was a secret between them. He was very careful not to tell Mum because Nan might be in trouble. Or Grandad!

Grandad could touch the ceiling and Nan's head reached his

shoulder. They both had wrinkly faces and their eyes twinkled behind their glasses. Nan's hair was grey and curly but Grandad had a bald spot that he tried to cover with white wisps, and their hugs were big and special.

Sometimes Grandad played tricks on Nan. That hot day last summer — Phillip always laughed when he remembered it. As he sat at the kitchen table drinking a glass of scrumptious lemon cordial, Grandad's big, bobbing shadow filled the doorway. He was as quiet as Jellybean, the cat, but Phillip knew he was there. So, when he called from the step, 'How about some of that for me? It's stinking hot out here,' Phillip had already handed Nan a glass.

'Come and sit down, George, there's no need to push yourself,' she said as she poured him a drink. 'But please, don't put that awful old hat on the table!'

It was a grubby, faded blue, raggedy old thing that Grandad loved to bits. He grinned at Phillip then he popped it on Nan's head! She pretended nothing had happened. Phillip giggled and giggled and didn't dare look at her. Grandad gulped his cordial then poured some more. When he finished he hobbled to the door, and guess what! He took Nan's straw sun hat from the hook and put it on! It had a pink flower on the crown and ribbons to tie under the chin. Grandad twisted them in a huge bow and strolled away to the garden while Phillip and Nan laughed till the tears came.

But it was different now. Nan hardly spoke to him and she didn't smile with her eyes any more. Nothing went right these days, like the time he tried to weed the garden and he pulled out carrot seedlings by mistake. Nan went spare, and next visit he found a padlock on the tool shed door.

As they drove to Nan's house Dad sang the worst ever songs that made Mum laugh while Phillip slouched in the back seat wishing like mad that the car would break down or even have a little crash so Mum and Dad couldn't go to that stupid birthday party.

After Dad parked in the drive, Nan opened the door. From the car his mother called, 'We won't stop, Jane — running late. Thanks for having him. Have a nice weekend, both of you.'

As Philip slid from the back seat clutching his bag she blew him a kiss but he pretended not to notice. When Dad reversed to the street Philip blinked hard to stop silly tears coming and gave a little wave, but when Jellybean strolled from her garden hide-out and rubbed against his legs he couldn't stop one or two little drops from trickling down his cheeks.

'Well, you'd better come in, Philip,' Nan called. 'Take off your shoes; put your things in the bedroom. I'm busy so perhaps you can find something to do.'

He knew it would be like this. I wish you were here, Grandad, he thought. He wandered around the bedroom looking at photos of Dad at College and with Mum before they got married. The house was very quiet. He supposed Nan was in the kitchen but he felt too scared to go there to talk to her. What if she shooed him out or was grumpy? It was while he was thumbing through one of Dad's old books that she called,

'Tea's ready, Philip. Wash your hands, please.'

Sausages with gravy and mashed potatoes were his favourite, but the broccoli stuck in his mouth like a lump of soggy paper and made him gag. Nan didn't seem to notice. Before Grandad died he sat beside him at the table and winked as he sneaked vegetables from his plate. Tonight Philip struggled not to cry as he nibbled tiny pieces of broccoli until his plate was empty.

Nan picked up a serving spoon. 'There's steamed pudding for dessert, Phillip.'

'No thank you, Nan. I think...' His tummy felt strange, tight and uncomfortable. 'Can I watch T.V?'

'Well, alright, but don't change the channel. The News'll be on soon.'

As he plopped into the big chair by the hearth he caught the faint smoky smell of Grandad's pipe. They would read wonderful stories about dinosaurs or wild animals like lions and elephants in this chair after Grandad had finished his evening smoke. Before Philip could turn on the TV, Jellybean padded into the room and settled herself next to him. She was so warm and soft, purring her pleasure at finding him.

When Nan came into the lounge she scowled.

'Did you encourage that cat?' she asked. 'I don't want it on the furniture!'

'No, no Nan, I didn't. She just jumped up. Poor Jellybean. I think — I know — poor puss, she's so, so lonely.'

The word stayed in the quiet room for ages. It seemed like they were all waiting for something to happen. Then Nan walked to the window and stared into the darkness.

At last, as he tried to swallow a big lump in his throat, Phillip whispered, 'Can I go to bed now, please? I — I'm…' He didn't add, 'I'm sad and I want to go home and I miss Grandad and I don't like it here anymore.' He scampered along the hall, fell on the bed and cried into the pillow, feeling like he was the saddest boy on the planet.

The next day was the absolute worst, most boring day of his whole life. For a while he kicked a ball around the yard. Then he watched a line of ants as they scurried along the path. Grandad could whistle like a bird so he practised that until his lips ached. Rain pelted down in the afternoon. He worked on his puzzle in the bedroom until Nan insisted he have a bath. Somehow the bath mat got soaked and he heard her grumbling about clumsy, useless children.

After he went to bed, he began to hatch a plan to run away. If he waited till Nan was asleep he could creep out of the house and go home. It was a long way but if he walked all night he might be there by morning. Anyway, if he got tired he'd curl up on someone's doorstep. A kind lady would find him and ask him in. After she phoned Dad she would give him a wonderful breakfast of pancakes and maple syrup, then a cup of tea with four spoonfuls of sugar

When he opened his eyes he was surprised to see sunlight through a gap in the curtains. Coo-ool! Today Mum and Dad would come! He pulled the duvet under his chin and imagined how it would be in his own bed, good smells of toast and bacon coming from the kitchen and Dad's shaver whirring in the bathroom. In the apple tree a thrush whistled to his mate. 'Grandad!' Phillip gasped, and in the same breath, 'It's only a bird, silly!' but there was something so cheerful about it that Phillip felt happier than he had in a long time.

An odd noise made him sit up. At first he thought there was someone outside. Then he realised it was coming from Nan's room. She was crying! Maybe she's got a tummy ache, he thought, or she's had a bad dream. He opened a book and tried to read, but the sounds went on and on. He began to worry and wished that Mum was there.

At last he knew he had to do something. He ran to her bedroom door and peeped in. She lay in the big bed, her wrinkled face wet with tears.

'Nan, what's wrong? Why are you crying, Nan?'

She turned towards him, her face worriedly-loving, the way she had looked while she watched Grandad when he was sick.

Then she reached for the photo that stood on the table beside her bed. There were tears on her cheeks but the corners of her eyes crinkled in a smile as she gazed at it. She wiped her face with the sheet and whispered, more to herself than to Phillip,

'Oh dear, you're so like him. Did you know that?' She sighed and closed her eyes for a moment then she moved to the middle of the bed and patted the pillow. 'Come here, Philip. You'll get cold, standing there.'

He hitched up his pyjama pants and began to walk slowly towards the bed but when Nan pushed back the duvet he rushed across the room and scrambled under the covers. The pillow smelled so good, like the flowers he'd helped Grandad cut one day last summer. After tea he had given Nan a hand to tie them in bunches ready to hang in the shed to dry. His thoughts were interrupted by something moving at the foot of the bed. There was Jellybean! She sat straight, her tail tucked neatly around her paws, her eyes almost closed.

'Look, Nan, I think she's smiling at us!' he whispered.

'Yes, I do believe she is,' said Nan. And she made no move to shoo the cat away.

Philip snuggled closer. Nan was warm and very comfy. Everything suddenly felt right, almost like it used to be. He started to laugh.

'D'you remember, Nan? D'you remember that day?'

White Sunday – Debbie Newlove

Our bus winds around the island's narrow roads, passing through the now familiar villages, one grand church after another — catching blasts of lush music, congregations in full song — as we make our way to the ferry terminal.

It's White Sunday and the day of our departure. Elisapeta, from our beach resort at Salelologa, has explained White Sunday to me. It's a day to celebrate the children. They get new white clothes and will be served first at the feast later in the day, after church. On this day they have no chores to do and tomorrow they have the day off school. Elisapeta had already laid out the new white clothes for her little girl, just three, and her baby son. She bought them from the market yesterday, but she has to work today so is gone before they wake to find them. I noticed her crying this morning, quietly to herself, as I passed by her desk on the way to breakfast, before we checked out and caught the bus on our journey home.

Elisapeta has the languid gentle grace and rhythm of an Island woman with an accompanying air of strength and solidity. She is light on her feet but can lop the top off a coconut in one efficient swing of her machete. It is she who took me aside a day or two into our stay to discreetly but pointedly let me know my elder daughter's clothing, (short) shorts and halter neck sun tops, while fine in the resort and around the pool, were not suitable attire out in the villages. The local culture remains fervently religious. Her entirely simple suggestion of a sarong is not necessarily so to my daughter's mind, however.

'Can't you go home for a while at least, to be with them?' I ask. There is hardly anyone staying now. But she says no, it won't be fair for the other staff if she has the time off. They all work such long hours, sleeping on mats in the hot part of the day, taking a rest when they can.

So we make in reverse the same journey we made exactly one week before. Back to another term of school, another round of work; clients, meetings, a Wellington winter.

We are happy to see the larger, relatively luxurious ferry in dock this time. The two ferries, one large, one small, cross in alternate sailings between the islands of Savai'i and Upolo. This one has an actual indoor cabin with air conditioning, food, drink and toilets on board. Such a relief compared to the stuffy little ferry we took on the way over. That one had been loaded down with trucks piled high with cartons of canned food, sacks of taro and other vegetables spilling out, and parked right up in front of the passengers, who were crammed onto just a few rows of wooden benches. There was barely room to squeeze past, and I worried if the trucks' brakes should fail... A tarpaulin was pitched overhead to keep out the meanest of the midday sun. The engine, so loud, droned on and on. I sat at the stern that time, my legs dangling over the edge, wondering whether I'd ever seen a sea so blue before. I was in awe of this vivid, vibrant place, so full of promise for the holiday ahead. I could barely wait to arrive.

This time, on the big ferry, the water is choppy, the white crests whipped up, and the ship pitches and rolls as the wind and current hit it port side on. Although we all took Sea Legs, we start to feel queasy, my kids and me.

There's a TV playing loudly in the cabin. It's a church service with expressive preaching and beautiful Samoan singing. It's obviously a special service for White Sunday. The children look stunning in their white clothes, garlands of waxy green leaves on their heads like crowns.

My stomach starts to churn and I feel my body heat rise. My mood drains low. The rumble of the ship's engines throb in my head.

A couple of rows ahead of us, sitting in one of the plastic orange seats, a large broad-shouldered, brass-haired woman gets to her feet. She lurches along the row of other passengers and makes a grab for the young Island girl who is wheeling her trolley with drinks and snacks for the ferry patrons, up the aisle. The brass-haired woman's husband, in a vivid orange shirt with tropical fish on it, follows in tow behind her.

'Stop!' She takes aim. 'I'll get some of that!' A broad Australian accent.

She snatches up, one by one, a selection of the foil snack packages until she has an armful. So many and just the way she does it: so entitled, so greedy. Satisfied, she leaves her husband to pay and waddles, laden, back to her seat.

My nausea grows. I am burning up. I feel a rivulet of sweat down the back of my neck. The voices around me sound muffled and I feel like I'm going to be sick. I get up, leaving the girls to fend for themselves. I have to get out on deck, to the fresh air, despite the heat. I lean up close to the railing and keep my eyes firmly on the blue line of horizon.

I notice another woman, about my age, maybe a little younger, also sitting out on deck. I wonder if she too is feeling unwell and needs the air. She is blond, luminously pale, pretty and petite, like a young Mia Farrow. She is perched daintily on the stair leading to the upper deck. I notice her clothes; a tailored linen skirt, close fitting, a smart, wide-brimmed sun hat and a red blouse. My own shabbiness makes an unfavourable comparison.

I don't feel much better, but I can just keep myself stable if I concentrate.

Make yourself small, very small. Let go of all tension in your body, just let go. Switch off your mind. Don't think at all. Forget the past, all you know or thought you knew about yourself. Don't think about the future. You are without a physical body; you are not anything at all. You are just one particle of light, maybe in the white clouds up there. You are one small speck in the cloud, just one light or water particle up there in the sky. Just existing. Just breathe and relax.

At last the wharf at Upolo looms close and we come into dock. We disembark and, clambering with our luggage, head off. The pickup area is vivid and bright, pulsing with heat, movement and colour. Multicoloured buses and vans manoeuvre; parking, loading and unloading luggage. A jumble of tourists and locals are coming and going; different languages collide.

It is tricky to wheel our luggage on small rollers across the ground which has been churned up in the recent downpour. I need to find the right shuttle amongst the throng. The one to take us to Aggie Grey's, our last port of call, where for the price of dinner we can fill in the day making use of the hotel's facilities until finally, tonight, we'll get a taxi to the airport and at an ungodly, early-morning hour, board our plane home. Then my girls are pointing frantically.

'Look! It's an owl. Over there — look!'

I look about bewildered. I can hardly comprehend what my kids are in such a state about. I can't see an owl amongst the throng. Why would there be an owl out in the middle of the day? And then I see, in a puddle of brown water, right in the middle of the thoroughfare, unbelievably, a mass of soft, white, delicately edged feathers, this beautiful creature.

I can make out the distinctive barn owl face, so perfect, but one wing is held outstretched, wrong, on a downward lean. It is slumped over like a broken toy, right there in the middle of the parking and turnaround area, where it will be run over at any time. Has it been hit already?

My younger daughter's voice rises urgently. 'Mum, what's wrong with the owl? Why is the owl out in the sun?'

I am afraid an inevitable tragedy is about to unfold. Why is no one doing anything to help this beautiful creature, so unusual a sight in these surroundings?

And then I see the pale, fair lady in the linen skirt, from the ferry. She is walking straight towards the owl. She goes right over and scoops it up, the heart faced owl, and she carries it cradled in her arms. Without fuss or hesitation, she has plucked the bird from the road where it was in immediate threat of being driven over and mercilessly squashed.

She is heading towards the grass in the shade by the water's edge. I'm so grateful to her for doing something for the owl because nobody else seems to care. What will she do with it?

I don't see where she puts the owl but then she is getting on the same shuttle as us, at the exact same time. I'm close enough to touch her arm.

'Thank you — for helping the owl.'

'Oh … oh yes,' she says and pauses, a look of absence in her eye. 'I don't think it will be all right though. It has a broken wing.'

We are pushed on with the other bodies and into what seats remain.

Nobody will do anything more.

Then I hear her before I see her, the brassy-haired Australian woman. She is outside, directing the luggage boys, pointing, gesticulating, making sure they are putting her baggage on the right trailer, attached to the right shuttle.

'Where's it going?' in her penetrating voice. Someone answers, but I don't hear what they say. And then her again, 'As long as it's not bloody Timbuktu.'

Much later, I am exiting the toilet cubicle at Aggie Grey's ladies room and find myself again in the company of the Mia Farrow lady. She's a step ahead of me, washing her hands at one of the white porcelain basins.

We greet one another, politely. We feel so badly about the owl.

'If I could have wrapped it in my shirt,' she says, 'and called someone. But who would take care of it?'

'Is there an SPCA?' I asked helplessly, uselessly, thinking of the beautiful creature.

'No. There's nothing like that here.'

Our gazes linger, then we shrug and continue washing our hands in the marbled washroom. It is all coloured tiles, pretty tropical flowers in vases, exotic shells, and neatly rolled hand towels in baskets woven from flax. We say our goodbyes.

I don't suppose I'll see her again.

I don't suppose the owl will make it.

Much later, my girls and I sit in the quiet marble lobby. Outside it is dark, though the stars are bright, intense. Frogs and insects murmur their background chorus. A huge chandelier of shells hangs marvellously from the high ceiling.

My younger daughter nestles against me on the couch, asking, 'What will happen to the owl? Will the owl be ok?'

I have to think hard before I can reply.

Moonlight Crossing – Deb Potter

The river was up when he stepped onto the swing bridge at twilight. He trod carefully, the weight of the pack threatening to shift his balance. On the other side, his boots anchored him to solid ground and the load felt secure again. He set off up the track with sure, ranging steps. Within minutes he had entered the bush and left the last of the light, but he didn't slow down. As he moved up through the tree line, he caught glimpses of the moon as it rose. He had struck soft pug in the lower valley, but the track firmed as he rose through the forest floor.

The beech trees were thick overhead. By day they made welcome shade after the first part of the climb, but by night he needed to use his headlight as the track became indistinguishable. The ground was covered with fine leaf mould. Over the tree roots hillocks of moss encircled each trunk. He'd come here with a girl once. Somewhere around this spot she'd gasped at the fairyland beneath the beech stands as he'd hoped she would. Before he tried to kiss her, she'd planted one on him. They'd shared a bunk that night.

He stopped to tighten his straps. As the pack shifted closer to his body its contents moved more snugly against his back. Straightening up, he inhaled the clean smell of water-logged moss and decomposing leaves broken free by his boots. He turned toward the head of the valley and moved on, the first step sinking slightly and the next making less impression. This place was special but it wasn't where he wanted to stop.

He'd done his first night tramp with his father, stumbling along until the old man had told him to stop trying to see the ground.

'Feel it. Trust your feet.'

And he had — right until he'd walked face first into his father's pack. Then his father had talked about listening too.

'You're an adolescent elephant. Just because we're walking hard doesn't mean you have to plant your foot with so much force. When you're an old codger you'll want to keep that effort for the hills.'

That first night tramp had opened Harry's senses to the bush. He was listening more than looking. He was feeling the track as his foot came down. As they'd walked on, his sense of smell told him how close his father was — oilskin and sweat just that little bit nearer. When the old man stopped, Harry stopped too. In the silence he felt his father's approval.

The terrain changed again, the beech forest gave way and the mountain cabbage trees let in a little more moonlight. It smelt different too, drier, and the clacking of the broader leaves in the wind made the world he sensed shrink around him.

This layer of the bush was over with sooner. The cabbage trees could take cooler temperatures than the beech, and they handled the wind too, but the track was still climbing. Minutes later the height of the vegetation dropped away and he stepped out of the trees and felt the ruts of the track, a spine along the top of the hill. The sting of Spaniard grass at his calves would have told him he'd reached the alpine level even if the night sky hadn't revealed it so clearly. It was like walking in a black and white movie.

Harry had made the full night crossing twice more after that. Both times he'd experienced a rush of emotion when he got to the tops and that happened again tonight. Some people were converted up here.

For Harry, the bush was like a church, easy to close the door on when you got back to clean clothes and arm chairs. He didn't mind the paradox of returning to atheism after a tramp. The old man used to say the Lord's Prayer every night as he'd tucked him in. *And forgive us our trespasses as we forgive those who trespass against us.* When had his Dad stopped doing that?

Up on the ridge the night was cold. Harry stopped. He rolled up his socks to shield his legs and put the headlamp in his top pocket. He was only going part of the way over the Crossing. Strictly speaking he wasn't alone yet — he was going just far enough to drop the old man off.

The moon was barely above his shoulder and the ranges were a frilled outline all around. The track was very visible now but experience told him not to trust his eyes — moonlight had a way of smoothing out the dips and ruts. Better to use his night sense and save his eyes for the view — a not quite frozen landscape awaiting the finishing touches of frost. *Magic.*

A fit man could make the walk up to the next hut in four hours and then on to the dress circle and down to Alpha hut in another five, but he was going to turn back. He'd thought about trying to buddy-up with someone and swap car keys half way, but it had seemed better to take the tramp alone this time. He shouldered his pack again. Moving off, he savoured the moonlight that, if the night stayed cloudless, would be his company until the descent.

The last time he'd done this tramp, he'd been with two other guys from the tramping club. There had been snow on the tops and the moonlight had bounced off it until it almost seemed like daylight. One guy had kept saying how happy he was and the only thing that would make him happier would be if his wife was here to share it. Since their bootlaces were frozen, Harry doubted the man's wife would be so thrilled, but he knew what the guy meant. On your own, the beauty was almost too much to take in. It would be good to be able to say something mundane to another tramper like, *Hard yards getting up here but she's worth it eh?*

He went on until he was mid-way across the tops. This was the place. He lowered the pack again and took out two flasks. The first was his tea. He poured himself a cup and took in the scene again. The world under his feet was untamed save a thin track where others like him had passed through.

He drained his cup and then took out the second flask. The bloke at the crematorium had enjoyed handing it to him. Too many people wanted fancy urns and boxes these days, he'd said. It was his Dad's flask — the thought of a cuppa from it had carried him up a fair few hills in his time. A fit old bugger, but the last few years Harry had seen he was getting on. A few too many nights outside in the rough might have given him the aches in his bones, or maybe they were always waiting to catch up. The cancer was well advanced by the time he'd gone to the doctor. Harry came over as soon as he was told. His Dad, although glad to see him, had said he didn't want Harry to think of him like this — wasted.

'Tell you what son,' he'd said, 'if you get the chance, take me up the tops one last time. Better still, leave me up there. I'd ask a mate but they're all getting on a bit now. You think you can do that?'

Harry opened the old man's flask. It was like he'd been waiting to get out as a small cloud of dust formed above it.

That was all they'd discussed of his death. The old man had been reticent as ever and Harry had felt he should fill in the silence so he talked a bit about his life in Canada, the girl he was seeing, the work they were doing, the times he got out into the wilderness — so much bigger and in some ways similar to New Zealand. He'd spoken of bears and beavers and then just sat and watched the life ebb out of his father.

A faint breeze came up and Harry stood with his back to it, letting it carry the old man further across the tops. He wondered if anyone would be around to do this for him and which country he'd most like to be resting on. He reached into the pack and took out the stones — they had added a lot of extra weight but he'd always known he'd be lighter on the way back down. He used flat round river stones at the base. They were stones they'd picked up over the years and added to their garden, along with the odd native plant they'd rescued on tramps like these. He put the old man's watch in the centre — it wouldn't last but he liked to think of it here. He poured out the last of the ashes. The next part of the cairn was formed with a few rocks they'd picked up from the Tongariro crossing — mouse-grey until they were wet and then they showed up a dark obsidian-black. They had the same shape as the river stones but their fine pock markings showed their volcanic origin. The rest, above those, were smaller and included a few bits of gravel from the driveway. The cairn was made of places the old man had gone and made a marker as good as any headstone.

When he was done, he kissed a last stone and laid it on the top. A bit of schist from Glenorchy. The pack was light now — only holding his sleeping bag and a few extra clothes in case the weather turned. He felt lighter too. He couldn't do much for the old man but he'd put him where he belonged. As he stepped away, he thought no, the old man had done this *for* him. He'd given him reason to come up here one more time.

He looked back at the cairn, now a silhouette on the closest ridge.

'See you old man, enjoy your view.' And Harry knew he'd be back.

He turned toward the scrubbier trees that straggled forward, trying to make a foothold on the ridge. With each footstep into the bush line, he felt his visible form bleed into the dark. He listened to the bush and felt the earth under each footfall and made it a fair way down before he snapped on his headlamp.

The trip down took less than half the time of the climb up. It was always that way. In the car park he pissed against a tree before chucking the pack in the back and getting into the old man's Holden. The engine clicked over straight away. He put the heater on, pulled out of the car park, and listened to the tyres on the gravel. The headlights made a small world ahead of him.

Overboard – Blair Polly

'A pint of lager thanks,' I said to the barman. 'Can't believe how dry I am.'

'Just sailed in, have you?'

'Yeah, from Wellington via French Pass.'

The barman smiled as he placed a brimming pint in front of me. 'Welcome to Nelson Marina. Enjoy.'

I gave him the thumbs up, snagged a local newspaper from the stack on the bar and plonked myself onto a stool. The crisp flavour of the lager filled my mouth.

'Ahh…' I said, wiping the light suds from my upper lip, 'that's so good.'

About halfway through my pint, I heard a loud burp to my left and looked towards the far end of the bar. A scruffy and very inebriated-looking man glared back at me.

'Who … who the fuck you looking at?' the man said.

What was it about harbour-side bars that attracted these guys?

I averted my gaze and hoped his addled brain would forget me. The last thing I needed was a hassle after sailing solo for eighteen hours. All I wanted was a peaceful drink before going back to my sloop and climbing into my bunk.

'I said, who you looking at, you ponce? Yes you, with the fancy windbreaker.' He got to his feet and wobbled towards me. 'You think just cause you've — cause you've got a flash yacht you're better than me?'

I could almost see the chip on his shoulder.

'Come on, mate, let me buy you a beer. I'm just trying to have a quiet one here. I'm not looking for trouble.'

The drunk lurched closer, a low growl emanating from his throat. 'You think I can't afford my own fucking drink, you wanker? I'll have you know —'

His words were cut short when my fist connected with his jaw. He staggered back, tripped, then fell onto the brightly patterned carpet and lay still.

'Ouch,' I said, giving my fist a shake. I looked down at the man and tried to justify the punch — there'd been no point in waiting for him to take a swing at me. He might have got lucky and connected. A fight was inevitable. Better to end it quickly, finish my drink and head off for some sleep.

Then I stared at my reflection in the mirror behind the bar and admitted the truth. He shouldn't have called me a wanker. Only my elder brother, Johnny, could do that. 'Wayne Kerr' had been his pet name for me. My real name was William, but various members of the Kerr family had been nicknamed Wayne over the years. Ever since Johnny's death at sea two months ago, being called a wanker set me off.

Keen to be back onboard before the lump of stupid lying on the floor woke up, I finished my beer with one long pull, looked at the barman and shrugged.

'Go,' the barman said, nodding towards the door. 'I'll call him a cab.'

'Sorry about that.' I slid my empty glass in his direction. 'I hope he doesn't cause you any trouble when he comes around.'

'My own fault. I shouldn't have served him those last couple of beers. He's been hammering it since his brother died.'

As I walked down the wharf towards my boat, I smacked the palm of my hand against my forehead. 'You moron! Why did you have to hit the poor guy?'

After a quick inspection of the mooring lines and fenders, I grabbed a rope and dragged the boat close enough to step aboard. Unlocking the hatch and flicking on the cabin lights, I took two steps down the companionway before turning sideways and resting my arms on the cabin top.

Lights reflected in the slight chop. The tinking of halyards and the slap of water on the hull of a boat to windward were comforting in their familiarity. As I surveyed the marina, I wondered if coming here had been a mistake. The last time had been with my brother, just before he set off to take part in the Sydney Hobart — before he'd been swept overboard in a storm that had been far more severe than forecast. The clip on his safety harness had failed when a huge wave swept the deck while he was on watch. The crew had done everything they could in the dark and treacherous conditions to locate him, but finally, with winds increasing to hurricane force, they'd had no option but to sail on in a desperate attempt to reach shelter.

I rubbed my swelling knuckles and thought about the loss of my brother. A one-hundred dollar piece of equipment had cost him his life. I shook my head and blinked away the tears.

A twinge of pain in my hand brought me back to the present. I wondered what happened to the brother of the man I'd punched. Had he been lost at sea too? Is that why he came down to the harbour to drink?

Ducking my head, I descended the last two steps into the cabin and pulled a bottle of rum from a small cupboard under the navigation table. Hoping a couple of swigs would dull the pain and help me sleep, I tilted the bottle to my lips. After a couple of pulls, I put the bottle on the table in the saloon and lay down on my bunk opposite.

But despite being dead tired, I couldn't sleep. Every time I closed my eyes, my thoughts returned to the man in the bar. Not only would he have to deal with his ongoing grief in the morning, he'd also have a sore face and monster hangover.

I reached for the bottle.

When I awoke the next morning, my lips were crusted together and my tongue felt twice its normal size. My head pounded so much I thought I was having a stroke.

Bang! Bang!

Then my brain clicked into gear. No, not a stroke. It was someone banging on the hull. As the gremlins played congas in my skull, I swung my feet off the bunk and made my way to the companionway.

Squinting into the sun, I poked my head above deck level and looked towards the source of the noise. The drunk from the previous night stood on the wharf, holding the guardrail unsteadily with one hand as he banged on the side of the boat with the other.

He stopped when he saw me, released his grip on the railing and stood up straight. His eyes dropped to the deck briefly before looking up again. 'I just came by to say sorry about last night. I don't usually attack strangers.'

His eyes were bloodshot. A blue and yellow bruise was beginning to spread along his jaw-line.

'Sorry, I went a bit overboard. I shouldn't have hit you,' I said. 'I should have walked away.'

'Yeah well … I can't really blame you. I've been such a dick recently.' His eyes returned to his feet.

'You look like you could do with some coffee. Want to come aboard?'

'Thanks. That would be great. I'm due at work in half an hour. I'm supposed to be water blasting and antifouling that forty-six footer in the slipway over there.'

I reached across and turned on the gas bottle that was lashed to a stanchion on deck and ducked below to put the kettle on. The yacht rocked gently as he stepped aboard.

'Come on down,' I shouted as I fiddled with the plunger and a couple of cups.

We sat at the table in the saloon, our hands wrapped around steaming mugs, and sipped our coffees in silence for a few minutes, relishing the bitter taste as it stripped the funk from our mouths.

'Sorry again for punching you. The barman mentioned why you'd been hammering it. I know exactly how you feel. I lost a brother recently too.'

'You did?'

'Hurts eh?'

He nodded. 'Technically, mine was a half-brother. We'd only discovered each other a couple years ago. My mum and his father had a fling. We'd met up half a dozen times when he passed through Nelson on various sailing trips. Apart from mum, he was the first real family I ever had. It was a shock when I heard news of his death.'

'That's so sad. What happened?'

Although they were red and swollen, he looked up at me with eyes that reminded me of my brother. A tear ran down his cheek. 'He was lost overboard during the Sydney Hobart.'

I nearly dropped my cup. 'Was his surname Kerr by any chance?'

'Yeah that's right … Johnny Kerr. Did you know him?'

I didn't know what to say. I obviously hadn't known my brother as well as I thought. I stared at the man opposite and wondered how I'd missed it. He was a year or so older than Johnny, but the resemblance was uncanny.

He took another sip of his coffee and smiled at me. 'I used to kid him and call him Wayne.'

Nobody's Wife – B.L. Stocker

I noticed the change in Karen the day she returned from Leon's crib. She breezed into our Manhattan apartment, her silver-blonde hair, normally slicked back in a tight bun, now loose and coming undone in soft curls around her ears. When she saw me seated on the red leather sofa, the newspaper held in front of me as I watched her from over the top of it, she touched her scalp and pushed back the wispy strands.

'Good trip?' I asked, my voice casual as if she'd returned from Bloomingdales or some other women's store that I had little time for.

'Yes,' she replied, touching her hair once more.

She kicked off her tan summer sandals then walked over to kiss my cheek. 'I'm going to freshen up,' she said.

'You do that, honey,' I replied. 'Then come back and tell me all about it.'

Karen went into the bathroom. I heard the squeak of the shower door opening and the rush of water throwing itself against the polished black marble floor. The cascade became uneven in tempo and I imagined her stepping under the stream, eyes closed, head tilted back, as she rubbed her hands over the fine bones of her face and pushed aside the clumps of water. A storm of blood surged through me and I flicked to the financial section of the New York Times. The Dow Jones had dropped 0.5% (something my broker predicted), with Merck contributing to the downward trend.

The drainpipe slurped.

I could not concentrate.

Karen had looked invigorated. She would be soaping herself by now. She had a good body, pale-skinned, perhaps a little tarnished by her fifty-plus years, but in all, trim and smooth. I wondered whether I would confront her when she stepped from the shower and run my own hands down her body. I also wondered if that was what Leon, my brother, had done.

'Bill — shall I fix you a drink?'

Karen stood in the entrance to the lounge. Her wet hair, curled into a knot, was held in place by a large silver clip, and she'd put on a pair of beige slacks and a loose fitting grey cotton top. She looked altogether dowdy compared with how she did when she'd arrived home. Perhaps she'd sensed that I wanted to make love.

'No thank you,' I said, returning my attention to the crossword in the newspaper.

'Do you mind if I have something?'

'Go ahead.'

Karen quietly disappeared into the kitchen. Her feet were bare and made no sound as they sunk into the plush Cavalier Bremworth carpet that I'd ordered in, all the way from New Zealand. When she returned, she held a glass of orange juice with ice, though I knew it would also contain a good measure of vodka. She stood there, sort of leaning against the doorframe to the lounge, watching me as if I were a curiosity. It was as if she were wondering how or when I would react — at what point would I lose my temper, or perhaps criticise her for forgetting to post the letter that I'd asked her to, even though I'd said I could do it if she didn't have the time.

'Are you going to have a seat?' I asked. I returned my pen to the breast pocket of my shirt, folded the paper and placed it on the coffee table in front of me. 'Come over here and tell me about your trip.'

Karen padded into the lounge and sat on the adjacent sofa. There was a new easiness about her, something about the way she casually placed her glass on the table then clasped her fingers together and opened her cupped hands so that she could study the inside of her palms. The tightness inside my chest grew and I wondered if things were going to unravel in a way that I hadn't predicted. I'd prepared myself for this moment, encouraged it, perhaps even instigated it, but all the same, Karen wasn't ashamed in the way that I thought she would be. She didn't come over and squeeze in beside me on the sofa, put her arm around me, and offer the apology that I was expecting for the time that she'd been away. She didn't do anything except appear to be bored.

'And?' I asked. 'How was it?'

'What would you like to know, honey?' she said, still staring at her palms.

'Anything — was Leon well?'

'Yes.'

'What did you two do?'

I'd like to believe that Karen blushed when I asked her this, though all she did was look up and study me with an expression that was neither alarmed nor confident, her blue eyes quietly scanning my face. I'd forgotten how sympathetic her eyes could be.

'This and that,' she said softly.

She looked away for a moment, at the terracotta-coloured apartment opposite ours on 73rd Street. When she began talking again, she returned her attention to me, though her mind was quite obviously somewhere else — probably still wandering those parched Wyoming plains where the wind flexed the grass, parting it like a comb.

'I helped fix up the crib,' she said. 'Cleaned up mostly, put things away, collected kindling; picked wild-flowers, went for a walk —'

She could have been rattling off a shopping list.

I nodded, wondering how long the both of us could talk around the subject though knowing full well that we would talk around it for the rest of our lives.

'The idea was for you to relax, Karen — not be Leon's servant.'

'Servant? No, Bill — I wasn't Leon's servant.' She smiled warmly and reached across the table to place her hand on my leg as if to pacify me. 'It was nice being there, taking a break from the city. Leon was a good host.'

I patted the top of Karen's hand then picked up the paper again and settled back into my seat. I pretended to be engrossed in an article about the drop in Obama's ratings and I muttered snippets of the text to Karen, though did not listen to her response. When it came to politics, Karen followed my lead and was inclined to agree with everything that I said anyway.

I turned another page. There was some sanctimonious dribble about gay marriages, then something about Ford cutting back on production, though, truth be told, there was nothing in that paper that could keep my attention.

I'd seen Karen pack a baby-blue negligee and I imagined her wearing it. She was lying in Leon's bed, the blue silk sliding into ripples to reveal the paleness of her upper thigh. The windows of the room were thrown open, the net curtains waving in the breeze, and the air rich with the sappy scent of conifers, the trees lying smashed and broken by the front porch, felled earlier in the week by Leon to expose the view of the valley below. There would be blue jays, perhaps a marmot nosing in the undergrowth, and Leon, standing in the doorframe of his half-finished house, his eyes upon Karen as she lay, her breath heavy from pleasure and from the pain that her actions had just brought.

I did not blame Karen for what she'd done — after all, I'd sent her there. Despite her Baptist upbringing, she wouldn't have been able to resist the tricks that my brother would have used to bed her.

'How's the place looking?' I asked. I put the paper to one side and gave Karen my full attention. 'Has much been done?'

'Just a little to the porch.'

'To be expected.'

I'd wanted to add that Leon wasn't particularly organised, or a particularly hard worker, but I decided to leave it there.

'Did you go anywhere nice for dinner?' I continued. Even if cash-strapped Leon had taken Karen out, it would have been to some burger joint where the meat was fatty and the lettuce limp. This thought tempered my anxiety. In fact, it made me feel a little smug. Of course Karen would never leave me for Leon.

Karen studied me as she sipped her juice. With her feet curled underneath her on the sofa, she seemed quite content.

'No,' she said, lowering her glass. 'We stayed in. It wasn't worth the drive to get a burger at some diner. It's Laramie, after all — not Manhattan.'

I massaged the stubble on my jaw and kept my face expressionless. 'I understand,' I said. 'Don't tell me that Leon made you cook?'

'No — he prepared trout.'

'Where from?'

'He caught it.'

'Was it good?'

'Yes.'

'Good.'

I was stuck on that one mildly unsettling word. Despite giving Karen everything that she needed, I'd never been 'good' for her. It was her catch phrase during the early years of our marriage: 'Bill — it's just no good.'

'Is that all you did?' I asked.

'I read my book, but yes, that was largely it. You know how much of a mess Leon gets himself into — there was lots to tidy up.'

Without knowing it, Karen had stumbled upon the essence of my brother.

'You're right,' I said keen to stress the point. 'That brother of mine, he makes a right mess of one thing before moving on to something else.'

Karen's eyes flicked to mine, questioning, though she didn't persist and let the statement pass. It was her ignorance that calmed me. She was still that naïve girl from Kentucky; that girl who somehow found herself pregnant with my child because I'd seduced her in the back of my Buick when she was eighteen and I was a much more worldly twenty-five. And it wasn't because Leon had wanted her that I'd got in first. I'd loved Karen, and by the time she lost the baby, we were already married so I got to keep her. I put her diffidence down to the stillbirth, and then, after years of trying, to the knowledge that she'd never carry full-term. It wasn't until that night in October, when Karen and I stayed in Leon's crib, that I learned that life with her didn't need to be so colourless.

'I'm glad you're back home,' I added, almost feeling pity for her and for the disappointment that Leon would bring. 'I was worried you'd find it strange being there without me. I would have liked to come — it's just that blasted Eric, needing those files at the last minute; and Leon, he was really looking forward to having us stay. It didn't seem fair to cancel the trip outright.'

'It's okay, Bill, it's okay,' Karen said, reaching over to pat my leg once more. 'I had a nice time.'

Then she picked up her glass and looked out the window again, at the neighbours who were preparing for a gathering on their balcony. They'd put up a sun umbrella and were arranging the patio chairs.

Karen and I had spent a lot of time at Leon's crib during the past two years. After doing my best to avoid him for most of my adult life, I'd decided, one random autumn day in 2011, that my wife and I should pay Leon a visit — as much to gloat at my successes as to survey what he didn't have. Leon was living in the foothills near Laramie, wrangling cattle when he absolutely had to, so that he could afford the gas for his truck, but for the most part he did as he pleased, the net sum of which didn't amount to much. I'd expected that first visit to be brief — that there'd be enough time to walk around outside and become bored as we blew steam through our nostrils and stomped our feet in some kind of Neanderthal way to ward off the chilling air. This was true to some extent, but what I hadn't anticipated was what happened when we came back inside. Karen became much more relaxed in Leon's presence, flirtatious even. She'd never moaned so much as that first night when we had sex in Leon's crib — an anomaly in itself, since Karen and I rarely had sex.

'You lucky bastard,' Leon said to me the next morning at breakfast as he studied Karen who sat, head down, at the opposite end of the rough-sawn table, her hands curled around her empty coffee cup.

I'd wondered if he'd seen us. There was a doorway to the guest room but no door.

Leon aroused something in Karen. Of that, I was certain. She'd been attracted to him all those years ago, before the evening when I sealed her fate in the Buick, and at first I thought she was tempting him by exposing a vivacious sexual need. So I waited. I cancelled the meeting that I was due to have back in Manhattan on Monday and extended our stay. Karen continued to be close, the sex was great, though she barely acknowledged Leon's presence, barely said a word to him. All that she offered him was a glimpse of her moonstone-coloured eyes that, for the most part, were directed at anything except his face.

Over subsequent years, Karen and I continued to visit Leon's crib and I began to make up excuses. I forgot the power cord for my computer, the batteries for my electric shaver, excuses that required the 2-hour return trip to town so that I could leave Karen and Leon alone. The pleasure I got from knowing that Leon was interested in my wife was immense, though not as immense as my pleasure in knowing that Karen would always be mine, regardless of any detour that she pursued. What actually surprised me was how long it had taken Karen to relent, though now, as I watched her quietly settled there on the sofa, sipping her vodka-spiked juice, I knew she'd crossed the matrimonial line. I waited for the guilt to surface and for the affection to flow. Karen was the type of wife who would commit adultery then repent for it for the rest of her life.

'Bill —' Karen began. She glanced at me nervously, as if suddenly perceptive to my thoughts.

I raised a hand to silence her.

'I mean it, honey,' I said. 'I'm glad you had a nice time in Laramie. It's just what you needed. You're a country girl at heart, and Leon, well, you've always seemed to get on well with him.'

Karen's face was troubled but I continued to talk past her.

'Next time we visit, I'll make sure that brother of mine goes to the same effort for me — none of those frozen TV dinners. I'll place an order for trout à la Leon. What do you say?' I reached over and gently brushed her cheek with my knuckles. 'It certainly does seem like the two of you had a nice time.'

Karen uncurled her legs and placed her feet squarely on the floor. She put her glass on the coffee table and pinched her lower lip between her thumb and forefinger.

'Bill,' she said. 'You don't think that —'

'Wait a minute, sweetheart,' I said, interrupting her. 'Before I forget — I have a client coming to dinner tomorrow night and I need you to pick up some wine. A red — something fruity.'

Karen stared at the neighbour's balcony.

'What's wrong, honey?' I asked.

It was only a matter of time before she would come over to the sofa and crawl into my arms. She would beg for forgiveness, the type of forgiveness that would take a lifetime to repay.

'I —' Karen began.

For a moment, I thought she was going to cry.

'I'd hate you to think that —'

Then, as if reconsidering, she turned from the window. 'How about a Stony River Merlot?' she asked.

'The 2013 Summercraft from Erkslee might be better,' I corrected. 'And now that I think about it, I would like a drink — vodka on the rocks. Do you mind?'

Karen stood without another word.

'And Karen,' I said, watching as her feet sank into the plush

Cavalier Bremworth carpet that I'd ordered in, all the way from New Zealand. 'I just want you to be happy. You understand that, don't you?'

'Yes, Bill,' she said as she stood there, her blue eyes flicking across my face.

'You'd never do anything to make me unhappy, would you?' I asked.

'No, Bill,' she said, before turning and heading back through the kitchen door.

Phillip's Face – Holly Painter

Phillip was born with a face. And so he was a freak. No one had a face anymore. People just didn't need them. Their brains had gotten so smart that they could see without eyes, hear without ears, and smell without noses. They could sing and speak and eat and breathe without mouths and they could show their emotions just by thinking about them.

Phillip could do all of this, too. But for some reason, he was born with a face.

The doctor who delivered him cringed. Not with his face, but with his mind. Phillip's mother felt the doctor's revulsion and fainted before she even saw her baby. When she woke again, the doctor put Phillip in her arms and she studied the strangeness of his face.

It wasn't a bad face. He had eyes just like the sky before a storm, pouty pink lips, and a tiny bump of a nose. It was a nice face, but it was a face, and he was the only one who had one.

The first time Phillip's mother took him out, all the people stared. Not with their faces, but with their minds. They crowded around the stroller and Phillip's mother could hear them jeering at her baby's little face. They'd never seen a face before and they thought it was gruesome and unnatural. Some of them even seemed angry and ready to hurt Phillip. His mother was frightened. She snatched up her son and ran all the way home with a hand over his face.

After that, Phillip's mother kept him at home. She taught him to keep his face still and quiet, and to talk and listen and see with his mind. She only let him outside in the winter, when everyone wore woolly hats like socks over their heads and no one would know he was different.

But the day came when Phillip couldn't stay at home any longer. He was a young man and he had to see the world, with his eyes or with his mind — it didn't matter. He just had to go. His mother begged him to stay. Phillip didn't remember the horrified people who'd surrounded his stroller as a baby, but his mother did. She feared what they would do to her son if they saw his face, so dear to her, but monstrous to anyone else.

But Phillip's mind was made up. He set off in the autumn with a sack over his shoulder and a hat over his face. He travelled through forests and over oceans. Alone in the mountains, he took off his hat and felt the wind on his face for the first time. He whooped at the top of his voice and heard it echo from the far-off peaks.

In the towns and villages along his way, Phillip met people of every description: runaway children who camped out in graveyards; tall, slender women who gossiped in twos and threes atop their elephants; rough, salty lighthouse keepers who played checkers with themselves. But he never met anyone like himself and he never let anyone see his face.

Soon, though, Phillip began to hear rumours of a man who lived on an island in the sea. A very old man. The last man alive with a face. In the spring, the fishermen would circle the island in their boats, believing it brought them protection and good fishing, even though they never actually saw the old man. No one dared set foot on the island or disturb the man with a face, fearing his primitive power.

As the winter snows began to thaw, Phillip made his way to the coast. He found a fisherman with a boat and asked to come along on the ritual circling of the old man's island. The fisherman consented and Phillip soon found himself aboard the rickety vessel as it joined the caravan of fishing boats parading out to the island. As the boat drew near to the sandy shore, Phillip made his second request of the fisherman. He wanted to land on the island. The fisherman baulked, but Phillip was insistent. Eventually, the fisherman agreed to drop Phillip several metres off from the shore, and he swam the rest of the way to the island.

It was not hard to find the old man's house — the island was not large, and it was the only house. Phillip was still dripping wet when he thumped on the door. He heard a crash from inside, and a voice — a voice like his! — snarling curses above the racket. 'Go away!' hissed the old man, 'You don't want to make me angry!'

Phillip hesitated. The voice was harsh, he thought, but he wasn't sure. He'd only ever heard his own. Peeling off his soggy hat, Phillip gently opened the door.

When his eyes alighted on the old man, he gasped and his gasp was returned. Phillip had never seen another face, and for the other man, it had been nearly a century. The old man swayed and Phillip helped him to a chair. The old man reached out and followed the wet curves of the young man's face with his fingertips. The wrinkly eyes widened, and Phillip wondered what it meant. 'Sir?' he said, out loud, and the old man's eyes leaked water down his cheeks.

'I never thought I would see another face,' sobbed the old man. 'I have my pictures, you see,' and he gestured shakily at photographs Phillip hadn't noticed before, 'but a face, a real face.' Phillip left the old man's side and roamed around the room, feasting on the shots on the walls. Couples, families, a whole army battalion of men with faces. He recognised the same people over and over, but with their faces arranged differently in each picture. Mouths open, closed, eyes narrowed or surprised, age overtaking the features as time pressed on.

'But how? All of these people...'

'You can't imagine the horror,' the old man's voice quavered, 'when the children started coming out faceless. They didn't know what was wrong. They thought it was the chemicals, the pollution. But then they found they didn't need the faces. They could do everything without them. And then we became the horrors. As more and more of us died, the few of us left became curiosities and objects of fear. I've been on this island for many years, all alone. They leave me alone because they fear me. But now? The faces are coming back?'

Phillip shook his head. 'No. I'm the only one. And they're still afraid.'

'Then you must stay!' declared the old man. 'You must stay here, with me. You will be safe here. They will not come for you. They will not hurt you. You will stay here, with me. And we will take care of each other.' The old man stretched his hand to Phillip's face again and smiled. Phillip smiled back.

And so he stayed on the island. He cooked for the old man and read to him from the old books about a time when everyone had faces. The old man taught Phillip how to whistle and wink and spoke of kissing and playing a flute with his breath. They spoke to each other out loud, and Phillip used his face to show emotion and learned to read the old man's face for feelings too. He spent months wandering inside and out, without bothering to cloak his face or keep it still.

Phillip was happy. They were a family. But he missed his mother and his hometown. He missed meeting new people and exploring new places. He tried to convince the old man to journey with him back into the world. They would be safe together. But the old man was still afraid, and he was weak. He had lived a very long time and the excitement and activity of having Phillip around was taxing his remaining strength.

One morning, Phillip woke to find the old man calling faintly from the other room. He was slumped in bed, wheezing softly, but his eyes sparkled from between his wrinkles. 'I wanted to see your face,' he sighed slowly and closed his eyes.

Phillip buried the old man on the beach, took a few of the old photographs and *The Iliad*, and rolled his head sock down over his eyes, his nose, and his mouth. He sat on the shore all night, signalling with a lantern, and just before dawn, a fisherman picked him up and ferried him back to the mainland.

It took Phillip months to find his way back home. He kept his hat snug over his face the whole time, though it scratched and smothered more than ever. Finally, one spring morning, he rushed through the doorway of his old house and wrapped his mother in a hug, her relief rambling wordlessly through his mind. He told her about his adventures, about the old man and his crinkled old face. He showed her how he could whistle and wink and brought out the photographs of all the faces. And he told her about the months he spent without the hat on, without hiding his face. That part frightened her. She could see what he meant to do, but she knew she couldn't stop him.

The next morning, Phillip walked out the door without his hat. He didn't know what would happen, but he couldn't stand to hide anymore.

That first day, he only walked around the block. His mother stood on the front porch, anxiously twisting her hands together, waiting. Out on the street, Phillip could sense the talk, the shock, the shudders of disgust. But no one accosted him. No one attacked him. When Phillip circled back to his mother's house, he was grinning. With his face and with his mind.

The next day, he walked around the block twice, and on the third day, three times. From then on, he sauntered through town every day, his hands in his pockets, whistling sometimes, quiet sometimes. Some days, Phillip waved and spoke a good morning to the people he passed. Other days, he just walked. After awhile, the talk died down. The people got used to the sight of his face and they didn't recoil when he came near.

In fact, as the months passed, Phillip began to make friends. It was slow at first. People didn't know whether to remark on his face or ignore it. They felt awkward around him, even though they were no longer afraid. But soon, they warmed to his generous heart and gentle ways, and Phillip became known as a good friend to have around.

Over time, one particular friendship developed into something more. In Anna, Phillip found a woman who loved him just as he was, and even the strangeness of his face became precious to her. Escorting her home one night, Phillip asked if he could kiss her. Anna was confused. She had never heard of kissing, and Phillip only knew of it from the old man's descriptions, but he tried. He grasped her hand and pushed his lips to the palm, then pressed them again on her cheek. Finally, he touched the place where her own lips would be, and kissed her there. With her mind, Anna smiled, and Phillip smiled back.

Through the Belgian Glass – Maggie Rainey-Smith

It was blowing a gale outside. From the comfort of her front room, Barbara stood watching a wedding party on the beach having their photo taken. Although she disapproved, thought a garden setting more suitable, she also worried. *What can we do about the wind?* She moved nearer to the window. As if by watching closely she could find a solution, solve the problem. Life for Barbara was a series of problems requiring her to worry on behalf of all those who, at any precise moment, might be suffering more than she was. And then she scratched viciously at the psoriasis on her elbow. Large flakes of thick white skin fell onto the carpet, and her elbow flared red.

'What a shame.'

'What's a shame?'

'They all look so jolly cold.'

'Who … who looks cold?'

Barbara's husband was reading the newspaper, comfortable in his new leather La-Z-Boy chair, not really listening to Barbara, but responding as he always did, by repeating what he heard — a reassuring echo. He'd learned that trick after years in the Public Service. Mirror the boss's body language, repeat what he says and he'll know you are listening. It hadn't been a spectacular career, but then he hadn't crashed and burned either, unlike others. No, in hindsight, he'd made all the right moves — a slow, steady and unspectacular career, and at the end of it, this very nice house with a view of the beach.

'Oh, no, she's going to get her dress wet.'

'Is it raining?'

'No, no, it's not raining. You can see for yourself!'

Impatience now in Barbara's voice, she rubbed her flaming red elbow, but she didn't take her eyes off the wedding party. It annoyed her — here they were with one of the best views in the Bay, and all Grant did was sit in his La-Z-Boy and read as if somewhere buried in the newspaper was the answer to life itself. Whereas Barbara knew that life was out there, on the beach, happening before her eyes and it was imperfect and it annoyed her and she wanted Grant to care as much as she did. She'd lived with him for forty years and, alone for forty years, she'd worried for the both of them. Promotions offered that he just missed, and then a sideways move with more pay and Grant happy for the chap who'd been promoted — because he didn't want the responsibility, not to mention the budget and you could never get it right, not when the minister came in and revised the policy around his portfolio at the drop of a hat. He'd never understood her aspirations for his promotion. Oh why did it have to be windy on wedding days — the poor girl, imagine all the planning, and the wind was going to ruin her hair. Mind you, her hair was pretty casual for a wedding. And the bridesmaids were in black.

'They're wearing black.'

Barbara spoke, but was unaware she had spoken. Her thoughts often came out as words and surprised even her.

'Who's wearing black?'

Irritation in his voice, Grant shook his newspaper, folded it, and tried to assume an air of interest in whatever was gripping Barbara at the front window. She was a thin woman. Was it any wonder after all that worry? A fine pair of legs, no visible veins, and not a bad bum either. But her face wore traces of worry like the skin of a very nice pear left too long in the fruit bowl.

'After all, it is a wedding and not a funeral.'

But she was talking to herself now. Now that Grant was showing an interest, Barbara didn't need him. She had lost interest in Grant's lack of interest. She was gazing with fond intensity at the wedding party, out through their new front window (a sheet of very expensive glass from Belgium). And then she rubbed, with her forefinger in a circular motion, at something on the window, as if the tiny spot she was rubbing was obscuring her view of the wedding. Grant was at her shoulder now, watching over it and out to the wedding.

'Poor bastard — bet he doesn't have a clue what he's in for.'

But she ignored him and kept rubbing at the spot on the window. He'd only said it to get a reaction and the lack of reaction annoyed him almost as much as her reaction normally did.

'I said, the poor bastard — I bet…'

'Oh look, look.'

He was looking because Barbara was rubbing the spot on the window with the hem of her skirt. She'd leaned down and lifted the hem up to the window, revealing her white and dimpled thighs. He admired the skin leaking from her knickers — her bum, once tight and white, less firm, but still attractive. He touched her. Right there, where the line of her leg grew in a soft curve outward and only slightly droopy below her panty line.

'Don't.'

She dropped her dress, forgot the spot she was polishing and carefully pulled the fabric over her backside, patting and stroking the material, the way Grant had intended to pat and stroke her bum.

'Don't be daft.'

Why did he always provoke her like this? This morning in bed she had tentatively fondled his foot with hers. But he'd been reading and had shifted his foot abruptly and sat up even further in bed, while she had curled foetus-like (knees almost up to her chin) and pulled the sheet over her head. And now, when she was here at her front window (who knows who could see her), he wanted to touch her.

A young man on the beach had lifted the bride into his arms and she was gripping him around the neck and the wind had entangled their clothes, their hair and they were laughing — it must be the groom, she thought. The man had long hair and wasn't wearing a tie — but look at the way he was holding her. Barbara's favourite movie was *An Officer and a Gentleman*. The best moment was at the end of the movie when Richard Gere carried Debra Winger out through the factory. Grant had lifted her once like that. Just once and even then he'd almost dropped her. It hadn't been romantic. She'd been worried she might fall. He'd been so reckless and tipsy and it hadn't been about her at all. He was trying to impress another woman at the time. Holding Barbara precariously (possibly even carelessly) and watching another woman — a dark, plump woman, who worked on the floor above Grant at Head Office. And even now, watching the wedding on the beach and thinking about Grant holding her to impress this other woman — her elbow flared and itched, and she scratched and this time her elbow bled. A large red teardrop sat on her elbow, it gathered momentum and fell and neither of them noticed a small red stain seeping into the new caramel-coloured carpet.

The wind picked up outside, increasing Barbara's concern for the bride and she'd extended her concern to the photographer now, who was directing the bridesmaids away from the shore-line and backing himself towards the water. Viewing the wedding through their new front window and with hindsight, Barbara was able to imbue her own life with not so much rose-coloured glass, but at least expensive Belgian glass. It was good to be worrying about someone else's future. And at that moment a rogue wave crept up on the unsuspecting wedding party, encircled them, washing their feet, spraying salt water on all their finery. Barbara felt panic for them, a physical shock that tingled down her arms and into her fingers. She watched and she worried at the window, and the wedding party doused in salt water, ruffled by the southerly, simply laughed, and laughed, and laughed, and the photographer, seizing the moment, stood back and carefully captured the chaos.

Memories: Sweet as Honey, Bitter as Lemon – Kathy Sewell

Charlie offered the leftover scrambled eggs to Clive, then sat at the table. He poured a cuppa and checked the newspaper's death column. There were no names he recognised. Relieved, he picked up the old faded, black and white photo, in the wood frame. Twenty young faces smiled back. Sixteen would never age, transfixed in uniforms forever on brittle paper protected by glass, ghosts from his past.

Clive barked with tail swishing backwards and forwards like a windscreen wiper as Pete, the caretaker of the caravan park, popped his head through the doorway.

'Morning, Pete.' Charlie stood.

Pete pulled a biscuit from his pocket as Clive stood on hind legs and danced in a circle, tongue flapping like a pink, deflated balloon. Pete tossed and Clive jumped, caught the prize and ran outside.

'Get in here boy, or the guests will have my guts for garters.' Charlie pushed himself up from the table.

'He'll be fine. Thanks for raking the leaves. Much appreciated.'

'No problem Pete. I appreciate being appreciated.'

When Pete left, Charlie sat on the unmade bed and slipped his feet into sneakers. The back of the second folded over and he scowled. His index finger reached down and fiddled until the leather obeyed its command. He unzipped the black canvas bag and without being told, Clive jumped inside. Charlie opened the wardrobe and took out his best jacket. The medals on the lapel were reflected in the mirror. Instinctively, his old fingers reached up. Over sixty years they'd been pinned in that same place, the ribbons had faded, but what they stood for never would. Clive yapped.

'I'm getting there, boy.'

He patted his jowls with their annual splash of Old Spice from the bottle his late wife had bought him twenty years earlier. He closed his eyes and saw Lorna's face. Not the thin, gaunt features during her illness but the soft, sweet face that had welcomed him home all those years ago. His beautiful Doris Day lookalike that he loved more than any other woman he'd ever known.

He pulled an old cheese cutter cap over his silver hair, picked up the bag and stepped outside. He shuffled down the lane, shoulders hunched.

A plump lady with blonde hair pulled back in an untidy ponytail stepped out of the park kiosk and called.

'Good morning, handsome.'

Charlie grinned and shifted the bag to a more comfortable position. There was something about her that reminded him of Lorna. It was the eyes, neither green nor blue, yet kind with a twinkle that suggested a sense of humour.

'Greetings to you, sweet Julie.'

'You look smart this morning. Where's Clive?'

Charlie whispered, 'In the bag, pulling my arms out of their sockets. I swear he gets heavier every week.'

Julie took the bag and put it down.

'Don't worry, if any weekend guests complain about a dog in the camp grounds we'll ignore them.'

She unzipped the bag. It overturned and Clive resembled a hairy, tanned turtle under a black shell. When he saw Julie he sat, and raised his front paws. Charlie wasn't amused. He'd never begged for anything in his life and this latest trick Pete had taught Clive was embarrassing. Julie bent down and scratched Clive's ear, apologising for having nothing.

'I was wondering if you'd like to have your caravan moved closer to the ablution block in about a month?'

'Remind me closer to the time, Julie. In case I have trouble remembering.'

He laughed, picked up the bag, shuffled passed the office and out the gate. Clive trotted ahead. In typical doggy fashion he ran from lamp post to car tyre, to fence. He sniffed, found an ideal spot along the rickety pickets and cocked his leg like a furry tripod, his fourth leg raised in a salute of farewell to the threatening odour now covered by his own.

'Stay on the footpath. You'll look like a bedraggled floor mop if you run on the wet grass. It's unfortunate that you have short legs and a shaggy coat.'

Clive took no notice as he chased the autumn leaves fluttering like amber butterflies.

A lady sitting at a small table outside the dairy, waved to him. 'Good morning Charlie. Can I interest you in a poppy?'

'Is that what you call them? These days they look more like clover leaves gone wrong. Still, what they represent is important.'

He gave her the money and she pinned the poppy on the lapel above his medals.

Charlie picked Clive up and crossed the road. His hand reached out and touched the rough, sandpaper texture of an aged tree trunk. 'Hello old friend.'

The tree stood tall, branches stretched out in no particular pattern as though woven by a large, drunk spider. Solid and demanding, it had control, with roots refusing to be encased. Over the decades it had lifted the pavement until it resembled a miniature range of grey asphalt, ridges and gullies.

'We're survivors, you and me.' Charlie patted the trunk, like slapping a comrade on the back. He closed his eyes and inhaled.

'Damn.' There was no comforting scent of Lorna's favourite Gardenia perfume. Nine years since she'd stood here and straightened his tie and brushed lint from his lapels. He wanted to stay, but time was ticking on.

At the mall they rested under the monument.

'Hey, mister, is that your dog?'

The young boy carried a 'happy meal' bag, his other hand gripped by an older girl sipping coke.

'Nope, Clive belongs to nobody. He's friendly with anyone who feeds him.'

The young boy opened his bag and tipped a hamburger on the ground. Clive ran over, picked it up and snuck behind the monument.

The girl scowled, 'I'm telling mum.'

'But I told you chicken nuggets. I don't like buns.'

Charlie smiled. 'That's a nice thing you did for Clive.'

'That's a stupid name for a dog, mister. I don't like it. Where did you get those medals? They're choice. I've only got a hamburglar badge.' He pointed to the coloured plastic pinned on his sweat-shirt.

Charlie touched the medals on the lapel of his faded jacket.

'I got these during the war, long ago. I wear them in memory of friends. This week's Anzac. I'm marching in the parade.'

'I like Anzac, we get a day off school. You must be rich 'cause you've got heaps of medals. Did you kill anyone, huh, did you?'

The girl grabbed her brother's arm and pulled him towards a lady pushing a trolley.

Stupid name for a dog, probably is, but it's the thought that counts. Clive Barrington, my old buddy. Charlie closed his eyes. *'Get up that hill, get it right boys. This isn't a practice run, this is for real.' They ran, they obeyed, orange flashes, smoke, screams and men falling everywhere. Get it right boys! Get it right! How the hell was killing or being killed right? One minute Clive was running beside me, the next his blood and guts covered my uniform. Bloody Smythe, and his orders… Bloody war. Me running, pissing my pants and running, with bits of Clive clinging to me.*

He shuddered and touched his medals. Clive whined, stood on his hind legs and licked Charlie's cheek.

'Get down boy, I'm okay. Did you hear the kid, I'm rich. We do alright in our old caravan at the park, don't we?'

Charlie shuffled down the road to the R.S.A. He knew there'd be fewer comrades marching than last year but that wasn't the war's fault, it was a fact of life.

Guess we can't have it both ways. You go to war, fight, live, get medals and are forgotten. You go to war, you die and the whole damn country marches in remembrance.

'We are survivors enjoying time held in place by so many sweet memories and some bitter.' He sighed. 'Life's a funny thing, isn't it Clive?'

Clive didn't answer. He was too busy quenching his thirst at a puddle.

Sorry? – Paula Slack

Mia Pink scratched her turned-up nose, her *nez retrousse*. This she valued, with its sprinkle of freckles, alongside Lorikeet, who sang as she sharpened the scissors, offering now a retro hair cut short, sharp and swept across ones forehead for the world to see.

'Mmmm… I'll think about it. Give it deep and meaningful consider…' What a laugh, she thought. I'm beginning to sound like Mum.

'How about this new colour? Bit bright, bit light, too much hair or not enough there.' The girl with the ring at the end of a nostril shook her head and gave an earthy sigh.

'*Taisez vous*! Shut up, I only want a wash and a wave. That's all I can manage this week.' Pause. 'Thanks.'

'Going somewhere?'

'What's that? Yeah of course I'm going somewhere.' Already Mia had decided that going to bed after her eyes had been glued to the screen was in fact going somewhere. Being stuck at home while everyone was going out that night, no way would she tell the hairdresser, so she shook her long locks with their rounded ends. 'No streaks today thank you,' and the hairdresser grabbed the noisiest hair drier the salon possessed and turned it on full force.

2.

When she arrived home all her mother seemed to do was take a sneak look at her watch. 'C'mon it's Sunday. When I was your age it only mattered if you didn't go out somewhere on a Saturday.' Her face lit up. 'And it didn't have to be a male.'

'Thank you very much.' Mia sat twiddling with her I-pod. Then she threw her arms in the air, reached across, and turned up the drums, the noise of number one.

'Turn … That … Thing … Down!' Her mother marched across the room, leaned over then glanced at the easy learning French dictionary propped up on the dining table. 'Mmmm… *Parlez-vous français s'il vous plaît?*' Then Sally flicked her fingers through her pile of CDs followed by a hurtful silence.

Mia took two deep breaths. 'What's in the fridge Mum? Hey! What's that you're putting on? Not Cohen! I know he's still a sell-out but…' She always cringed when her mother got up and danced in the aisle. I'm not going with her again she thought, not to any of the ones worshipped by the wrinklies!

Meanwhile Louse, a lovely little Labrador, lay on the lino licking the last of the water. Mia really did adore him. It was just she had weird ways of showing it. This time she'd given up trying to make her big bro amend the error he'd made. Louse! A dog! 'You can't even spell,' she'd said. 'You left out the 'i'! Just how dumb can you get?'

'I like Louse,' he'd said. 'It's more pragmatic for a dog.' But Lenny wasn't really interested for by now his foot was usually flat on the pedal of his 1964 mini, a model quite cool with an air scoop and modified engine.

3.
He still owed his Mum half his pay from delivering pizzas. He scratched his head. Or was it his Dad who he'd short-changed.

#

At the same time, George Grimsky was feeling in a melancholic mood as he placed his head inside the oven. It was even worse than he would ever have imagined — almost as if the world was going in the opposite direction. Was that a deathly stench? He shuddered then quickly exhaled. With his pale blue eyes scarcely moving, with only a few peppery strands of hair left, his skin met a sharp edge and his face screwed up.

George often swore. This time it was as he wiped the blood, only a little, from his forehead. Then he smiled for he knew that later it would be a good opportunity to include some sadness for the reader, have reason for them to wipe their eyes, sniff or, best of all, for them to long to read more of the series.

His head, was it still resting on the oven tray? Nah, now for most of the time it hovered over screeds of paper while his pen was chewed as if he was canine. Sometimes he waved the papers round and round in the air. And on other occasions it was used to slip stupidity into his manuscripts, but often good sense. George Grimsky always lay awake at night writing. He drank coffee until the early hours.

'Goodness gracious me,' he muttered and switched on talk-back. 'Now they're saying that caffeine is said to help prevent Alzheimer's. Just think, the Germans and the Frenchies reckon a caffeine fix could perhaps be the answer and he sat up straight, threw his arms in the air, and sang his very own rendition of the lovely *La Marseillaise*. It always gives me feelings, he thought, again speaking to himself.

4.

However when his head fell back on his pillow, he remembered that the caffeine tests had only been carried out on mice. So very quickly he decided to postpone a jazzy *Three Blind Mice* rendition. Fantastic research, he decided, but perhaps I should wait until the preventive effect is completely evidential.

Once more George Grimsky fondled the ring on the fourth finger of his left hand and ran lean limp fingers through his beard where many shades of grey still rested. He was now half way through the draft of book number four, that sometimes he felt quite overwhelmed. What seemed to stand out to him was the more important question from one friend to another, 'Do you like me?' or 'Do you love me?' And why, so often he had discovered, there is a large wastage of life and effort in human experiences whether the time spent is bad or good.

Sleep started to come but he worried it would all have left him by the morning, so again he reached out and picked up his perpetual pen. Lights still twinkled from the tanker across the bay as his mind became alive and thought of new things to say. He looked across at the pair of puppets he'd brought back from Indonesia many years ago still sitting upright on the floor. Maybe I can find words of wisdom there.

Perhaps it is time for me to travel around again. If the Pinks are back together or still apart, I'd be happy to go with either of them to Lombok or Lickey Hills. But now I need some sleep. Thank goodness for boiled milk and ginger nuts.

#

Meanwhile, all this time, Walter Pink was earning his keep, thinking what the hell am I doing here? Celebrate the body beautiful with the best ever blobs of lovely lotion extra worthy of having in the sun. He faltered and, his mouth wide open, he stifled a yawn.

5.

When he began to read it out loud this time he started with a clever mix of fun and friskiness for beach wear, black purple red and a bright emerald with built-in bras and… and…

He yawned. 'After all it is primarily about shoe string shoulder straps.'

Walter Pink hated his job, being a salesman made him melancholy. He longed for his fishing line and the clear water into which he'd soon thrust his new rod. What else? Perhaps a parrot, yes a parrot. He was sure there was still room for a Polly in the porch at the back of the house. Their budgie, a beautiful blue, was always good company when his Sweet Sal used silence for 101 reasons.

Pity she didn't stay quiet when he refused to bring home any of his catches for tea. His wife had never understood 'catch, weigh and then back in the river they go'. Without warning, his ears began to itch. Next he scratched his nose where the sun had been shining in the middle of the day. Well he thought all sorts of reasons — that's what they always say at the doctors, and his lips shivered. Once more, he sorted his body beautiful notes then shuffled from left foot to right. Back at home his rod was ready, his bait was waiting, but was he?

Suddenly he heard an angry screech. It was then he saw the bundle of sparkling green paper with the words ECOLOGY GREEN KEEP THE RIVERS CLEAN scrawled all over it, rather like a flag flying from a plane not from a fishing rod. And on the other side of the river, right at the edge, was a myriad of anger with eyes ever keeping watch over him as if to say, 'I am going to get you Mr Pink!' It was the fiercest bull he'd ever seen in his life. A bull that was often responsible for not keeping the rivers clean.

6.

Hallucinations! Could it have been a dream? Or did the bull intend to place fear inside everyone who passed this way? Walter Pink parted his fingers and peered through. But the bull had bolted.

#

'Mum!' But Mia didn't have to say much more because her father's face was unbelievably happy.

So she sat there and wiped her eyes with pink paper towels. 'I'm all stuffed up,' she said. 'Daaad! Mum and I went on the ferry to Devonport during the weekend. We saw this unbelievable second-hand bookshop, y'know the one with the dungeon that was used for protection of people during World War II.'

'Ah! *Faire la guerre*, to make a war'. Mrs Sally Pink shook her head.

Meanwhile her father had made the big decision. Finally he'd decided to forget the fashion show for females with imperfect bodies. Are they not all like that? He still loved his Sally but sometimes looking at her reminded him of solid and large, but after all they'd only recently separated.

Nowadays she'd say, 'We see more of you than when you lived here.' No, he wasn't really sure which way he'd go, her too. She'd keep the cat. The cat named Mouse. And she'd keep on nagging that Mouse, after all, was hers.

7.

At the same time George Grimsky was convinced that all things must be appreciated, and liked. Without a doubt, and not far away, some people may criticise. Some would push how all worthy people know that if there were no writers there would not be any written words. He sighed. Happy birthday, Mr Grimsky. Now George, just because you hit the half century you do not have to roll over and play dead. He shook his head. Was that me speaking? he wondered.

What a place to have been — introducing my third bestselling book to the best bookshop in town. As the woman who introduced him had said, 'Mr Grimsky, you didn't fall at the third hurdle.'

#

'Mum's leaving!' Mia's voice broke the silence until without warning she whispered, 'Dad!' But Mia kept looking at her watch. 'Did you want to talk to her? Or are you guys still not communicating, talking. Hey, why don't you?'

'You are referring to your mother.' He yawned. 'Me. Communicate?'

8

Walter Pink flushed as his teenage daughter responded loudly, 'Open up, get together again, mean sorry, forgive, forget, open up...' Mia didn't raise her head but she was grinning from cheek to cheek as she saw father's florid face.

'Okay, okay you don't have to go through it all again,' Walter warbled loudly. Who now considers himself to be a separatist greenie, still unsure as to where he should place his vote, and no longer instrumental whatsoever in selling women's lingerie AND with rotten pay. Again Walter yawned, opened his mouth wide. 'Coffee?'

Mia squinted. 'Milk no sugar. Mmmmm… So I'm getting it. You need a change — something new. A challenge, the whole works, where you'd both meet nice and interesting people, Dad and don't forget! You're not getting any younger.' Mia turned, then covered her face. 'Mouse … Cat … Louse … Louise.'

Her father smiled.

She said, 'And Dad, I'll promise to forget you always used to lecture me never to resign from a job until you have another signed up. And Listen. *Vraiment gentil.*'

'Cut it out,' said Walter. 'What the heck does that mean, Sal?' He snorted as she made her way back into the kitchen. 'Forget something?'

Biting her lip, his wife began to roll her eyes. Then she said softly, 'Sweet as.' She flicked her fingers and said, 'I'm going out.'

'Me too, be empowered Dad,' whispered Mia. Walter thought he could see something special on her face, but when he looked again, she'd gone.

9.

'Sally! Wait! Don't go! My resignation's gone. I've sent it off. You are right you know, not everyone will like it but you know me. I just strive for confidence,' and he wiped his tongue over his lower lip then laughed. 'Even the musty smell of a used book to sell would make me feel good.'

Sally turned, grinned. 'We need to find George Grimsky Esquire. There was a big write-up about him in the papers, over the air too. Shows you what you can do if you don't give up.' She frowned. We should have gone, she thought.

'Yeah he's certainly kept going. For a while it was rejects and more rejects. And now look!'

'Late nights, no nights — he was quite funny yet funnily serious if you know what I mean,' she said. She turned to go. And this time she wasn't coming back until he'd walked out the door.

But just then Lenny blew inside. 'G'day! Dad! Didn't know you were here. Could you have a look at my engine? Like now!'

'Why aren't you working today? Thought you were doing regular deliveries while you're at Uni,' said Sally.

'Oh I am. What are these CDs doing here? Interesting, some of them are starting up cool again. Bit like you guys,' and he grinned. 'Yeah, thanks, I've got time for a quick snack, Mum.'

10.

'Look at all these, Dad — Elton, Bee Gees, Beatles, Queen, old Michael Jackson. I can use my bike for now. Thanks, Mum.'

'See ya later everyone. Gotta move.'

It wasn't long before Sally and Walter Pink were curled up on the couch while Cohen crooned. Walter Pink provided egg sandwiches with thick crusty brown bread and a little thinly sliced lettuce. Then he disappeared and turned up again with a pile of books and a 2013 Albarino. 'I picked up the reading matter at an auction — one of those nice old houses round the corner from here.'

For a while he hid his face in the daily paper. Then he played around ready to make a start on how he'd arrange all the cartons of second-hand treasures. When he opened up the cardboard boxes, they were full of books at the beginning of a new life.

Later that night, together, they battled the winds, passing the musicians in the seedy part of the city they loved. Most men with their hats hanging upside down waited for coins to clunk and hit the mark and some were very good, others not so. But at least they tried and the music made the whole scene come alive.

'S'cuse me!' an old man would say. But while some answered with pizza, pie or piles of coins, others chose to turn the other cheek. Walter reached down, then clasped Sally's hand.

11.

Back home he said, 'I can't believe we're going to start a second-hand book shop. Our very own shop with cafe and music, CDs to sell with tables and seats — wood of course — on the pavement outside where everyone has a place to read and talk and even listen.'

Her green eyes twinkled. 'A lot of people just like to watch the world go by.'

'I'll stay with you tonight,' he muttered, taking a quick glance. 'We really must be together — the lawyers will need both our signatures tomorrow morning.' And his voice said huskily, 'Did you ever read how Solomon said that a friend means well, even when he hurts you?' He winked, 'Like the time…'

She leaned across and planted him a crazy kiss.

'Then C'mon Friday,' he said. 'Wow! We're all going to be so busy getting our stock in, but the kids can help. They can fit it in with their studies — do them good! I'll get started on the shelving. Do you think anyone would buy my date and orange muffs?'

As she sped through the doorway, it was Mia who chuckled and nodded her head. 'I'm okay with egg and lettuce sammies. You could do the dishes, Mum.'

'Fun-ny!'…

12.

Walter, on most mornings, was the one to choose a book and place it on the seat opposite in the shelter where buses stopped.

And it brought back memories of their own O.Es. Done early in life, together, and how they'd met George Grimsky on the train from Paris to Prague. It was a first for them, to pick up well-read books from a bus shelter then drop them back later on, often in another country.

Everyone had been over the moon when George Grimsky had been able to remove his head from the oven, and again when his third book was published so successfully in the year. He himself told the story about trying to give his oven a clean and getting his head stuck. How he'd expected his chest to explode and how he sweated and his throat felt it was full of bile from the smell of the build-up of congealed fat.

Now home again, at the opening of the Pinks' second-hand-cum-cuppa-coffee bookshop with New Zealand-made camellia tea at the top of the list, George also talked about his time abroad and his third bestselling award-winning book *Tout Le Livre*. Everyone clapped.

'Signed copies for sale' cried Lenny. 'Even though *Tout Le Livre* isn't what one would call second-hand.'

'Well not yet,' laughed the author and in the background Mia set up her Mum and Dad's fave, Whirimako Black, with a soul session of *What a Difference a Day Makes*.

How I Found My Father – Brindi Joy

I'll begin this story, though it doesn't begin here. This story began long before I was born. But this part — the few links in the chain that connect my life and my father's life for a brief moment — begins with the ringing phone.

Behind us, Mom's old Pontiac ticked as it cooled in the driveway. We'd just gotten home from my high school graduation and I was desperate to get inside and cool off. Arizona's summer sun is unrelenting and I'd been in it all day — a sun magnet, in my black cap and gown.

Mom fumbled with the keys in the deadbolt. *She's thinking about Dad again*, I thought. I didn't ask her to talk about it. She wouldn't want to. Talking reminded her that after all these years she still missed him. She sighed, dropping her hands to her sides. 'Show me again,' she said cheerfully.

I opened the maroon leather-look folder for the tenth time.

Mom cocked her head as she read the document again. Her brown eyes shone. 'Jonathan Stauss. Class of 2004! We'll frame it, Jon. Tomorrow I'll get a frame at Target. We can hang it over the mantle.'

'All right.'

She pulled me in close, giving me a soft mom-hug. I like those. Even though I tower over her. I picked a rhododendron blooming magenta beside the stoop and tucked it behind Mom's ear. She'd told me once that she and Dad had planted a garden together. There were rhododendrons there, too.

Mom turned back to the door. Her hands began to shake.

'Here, Mom.' I eased the keys away from her and in one motion unlocked the heavy wood door and swung it open. A welcome wave of air-conditioning rushed my face.

That's when the phone rang.

She didn't stir. She stood staring through the open door, unmoved by the phone's shrill urgency.

'The phone, Mom.' I indicated toward the kitchen.

She swayed slightly and stepped inside, her flowery dress swishing around her ankles and her white sandals slapping against the floor. 'Hello?' she said. 'Hello?' Her face changed. The receiver fell from her hands and bounced by the spiral cord inches above the linoleum.

'Your … your … father …' she breathed.

The rhododendron dangled precariously from her ear.

I picked up the hanging receiver.

I asked Mom if she wanted to come with me to New Zealand. She was sitting on the couch in the living room, a glass of Lipton iced tea in her hands. The ice clinked as she looked away from me.

'Just one phone call and you're on a plane? You're going?'

'Yeah. I've got some money saved. You wanna come?' I asked again, knowing she'd refuse, but still holding out hope for a yes.

She looked so frail just then, so broken. She merely shook her head. 'Turn on the radio, will you, Jon?'

All right. End of discussion.

I leaned over the couch and switched on the transistor radio she kept there. Mom began to sing. Her voice and John Denver's rose and fell in unison, as if he were still alive and singing songs and not scattered somewhere over the Rocky Mountains. *Country Roads, Take Me Home* had always been her favourite.

'I'm going to find my father,' I told the old lady sitting next to me a few months later. Air New Zealand Flight 19. Los Angeles to Christchurch. Non-stop. Hour ten — three and a half to go.

She turned to me, her creased face kind. She smelled like a grandma — her clothes like lemon drops and her breath like mint ice cream.

I adjusted in my aisle seat. No chance of seeing the scenery on the way down. 'The Christchurch artist, William Stauss? Ever heard of him?' I asked.

When I told her where I planned to meet him, she said with certainty, 'You won't find him there, dear.'

I stood alone outside the arrivals terminal, the toes of my beat-up New Balances hanging over the concrete curb. The Christchurch Airport looked like any other airport I'd been to. I'd have to take the pilot's word that I was now standing on an island at the bottom of the world.

I considered: not the parked taxis, shuttles and buses lining the airport façade, or the fact that I was halfway around the world; I was thinking about my dad.

'Need a ride, mate?'

I turned expectantly toward the voice. A weathered taxi man leaned against his white cab.

I sighed. Of course it wasn't Dad.

'No, man,' I replied. 'Can't spare the cash.'

The taxi man smiled, showing me the gaps in his teeth. 'Suit yourself.'

Shouldering my backpack, I hopped on a bus.

'Where ya headin'?' I heard behind my head.

I turned in my seat to see a scrawny kid about my age. A behemoth of a backpack leaned next to him.

'I'm hiking through the Southern Alps. Where ya headin'?' he asked again. He sounded American, too.

I had three addresses in my pocket. I told him my first stop.

197

He screwed up his face. 'What a waste! One hundred percent pure New Zealand and you're wasting your time with *art*?' He nearly spat the word.

The gallery on Victoria Street sprawled from sidewalk to back fence. Two sides were glass and I could see inside, despite a sudden burst of driving rain. I made no move to enter. Track lights illumined wood floors. Expensive-looking paintings hung on the long interior wall. There were no customers. A girl sat behind the reception desk. She was writing.

This was the kind of place where people who wore cashmere turtlenecks and drove BMWs or Mercedes would be welcome. Not a dripping wet, middle-class teenager in ripped jeans.

I began backing away, turning toward my hostel when I tripped and nearly fell backward from the weight of my backpack. I caught myself on a car. A Bug. A purple VW Bug. Not a Beemer. Defiantly not a Mercedes.

TKITEZ the licence plate read. Take it easy. I decided to try.

She must have spent her whole life smiling. When I got close I saw small lines that actually turned up at the corners of her mouth.

She stood up from the reception desk. 'Hello!' she said, though it sounded like no hello I'd ever heard before. Hello-er.

'I'm here to see Leon Glass,' I said, trying not to drip all over their floor. 'I'm —'

'Jonathan Stauss!' Leon emerged from an office in the back — a towering, middle-aged man sporting an impressive white moustache. He opened his arms to me and then hesitated. 'Look at that face! Just like your father's!'

My heart stopped. I stared. 'No … no one's ever told me that before.' I shoved my hands deep in my pockets, hiding how they suddenly trembled, like Mom's. When Mom had finally moved home to Arizona from New Zealand her luggage never made it. She had arrived on her parents' doorstep with nothing to call her own but a baby on the way. All pictures of my dad and her life with him had been in those two bags. 'I've never even seen his picture,' I said.

'Crikey!' Leon exclaimed. 'Wait here, Jonathan. Talk to Sophie. I won't be two ticks.'

Sophie smiled at me. I thought I saw a laugh hovering on her lips. It might have just been those smile lines, though. They made her look like she was always ready to laugh.

She must be my age, I thought. *Maybe a couple years older. Real pretty.*

'I'm glad you could come,' Sophie said, opening a line of conversation.

I couldn't reply. A sizable lump had begun to form in my throat the moment I laid eyes on her. Damn insecurity! I hadn't even gone to my senior prom, being too shy to ask any of the girls in my class.

'I've been looking forward to meeting you,' she continued, 'ever since Leon invited you to the exhibition.'

The phone call. I could say something about that. 'L…Leon called on my graduation day,' I said. 'He freaked my mom out. She heard his Kiwi accent and thought it was my dad. I think she's still recovering.'

'Here it is.' Leon re-emerged from his office. 'New catalogues haven't been delivered yet, but this should do.' He thrust an old art catalogue in my hands, pointing to a photograph on the bottom left page.

I couldn't speak.

For the first time in my life I was looking at a picture of my dad. He had pale, pale blue eyes. A unique blue 'gathered up from New Zealand's bluest glaciers,' Mom used to say — but she had been describing my eyes. 'Can I keep this?' I asked. I didn't want to study it then, in front of them. Later, when I was alone, I wanted to look at it and understand William Stauss at last.

Leon clapped me on the shoulder. 'Don't know who better it could go to, son.'

Son. I'd been called son. No man had ever called me son before. It sounded nice. Son.

Huge blank canvases had been transformed into sweeping landscapes — a spectacular copse of tall old trees, a bay of turquoise seawater, a mountain pass — with two or more people in each. The paintings exploded with colour and made me want to take long deep breaths to draw in the fresh air created by each brushstroke. Mom had told me once, 'Your father liked to paint.' She never mentioned that he could do *this*.

'They were boxed up in storage for eighteen years. Never collected,' Sophie said after retrieving the paintings from the back and leaning them against the gallery wall for me. 'Forgotten after he…um left.'

I nodded without speaking. Leon was taking a phone call in his office. I stared hard at those paintings, hoping to pierce the layers of paint to find some undiscovered truth about my dad. *What more is there?* I wondered.

'They're painted around Canterbury,' Sophie offered. 'Akaroa, Governor's Bay, Arthur's Pass.' She pointed to each painting in turn. 'Unlike other landscape artists, Stauss never suggests we're intruders on the earth. His paintings celebrate a *union* between humanity and nature.'

My focus shifted from my father's paintings to Sophie. I watched as these revelatory words fell so easily from her lips. 'How do you know that?' I asked.

'It's in the catalogue.' Sophie opened it for me again.

I hadn't seen the artist's bio:

> *William Stauss. 1957 – A proponent of the ideal that mankind can 'tread lightly on the earth,' Stauss infuses his work with a vibrant and heartening portrayal of Aotearoa. Stauss lives in Christchurch with his American wife. His first child is due at the end of the year.*

My legs couldn't hold me up any longer. I collapsed on the wood floor, trying to make the move look intentional and cool. Sophie sat down next to me, Indian style.

'This must've been printed when Mom was pregnant with me...' I trailed off.

Sophie reached out and touched my knee. My leg jerked. Stay calm.

'What do you think about the paintings?' she asked.

I turned back to the canvases, trying not to tremble all over. Now at eye level, I felt closer to them, to my dad. 'I don't know anything about art,' I said lamely, even though I imagined stepping into the paintings and becoming enveloped in their kaleidoscope colours. I didn't expect a reply, so I focused on the instrumental music pouring through the sound system. An energetic classical guitar and violins became the soundtrack to my father's paintings.

'You don't have to be trained in art to appreciate it, I reckon,' Sophie said after a while. It became obvious to me that Sophie was more than a receptionist. She loved art. Understood it. And was good at talking about it. 'Appreciate your dad's portrayal of New Zealand and then maybe a deeper understanding will come later.'

My jaw slackened and I looked at Sophie then. Really looked. Her deep blue eyes had a wide-awake spark that didn't once waver from mine.

Hoisting myself off the floor, I offered Sophie my hand. She looked surprised. So was I. But she accepted and stood.

'You can help me hang the show on Wednesday,' she said, disappearing through an opening behind the reception desk. I could see at least twenty sliding racks full of paintings back there. Sophie hung one of my dad's on the first rack and then re-emerged. 'Including these three, we have thirty paintings for the exhibition. Patrons from both islands have loaned work for our 'reintroduction' of William Stauss.'

No, thanks. 'I'll think about it.'

She picked up the mountain landscape. Moss greens and sapphire blues flashed. A man and his small son were neither dwarfed by nor dominated the mountain scene.

'The guests will love chatting with you.' She stepped past me with the canvas, stirring up a floral-scented breeze. 'People are coming all the way from Auckland.'

I shuddered. What would I say to them? Smiling and nodding would only get me so far.

'What's that?' I asked suddenly.

Sophie stopped.

Something on the back of the canvas caught my eye. A faded white label. I bent over to read it. 'William Stauss. Oil on Canvas. 1986. *My Son's Inheritance – Arthur's Pass.*' I wanted to cry.

'I want to go here.' I pointed to *My Son's Inheritance*. 'Sophie, how can I get to Arthur's Pass?'

Two days later, on Sunday, Sophie picked me up from my downtown hostel in her purple Bug. It stopped raining and the sun shone close to the earth and bright in my eyes. Perfect day for a road trip.

'You ready?' she asked.

'I think so.'

'Hop in.'

I was greeted with a face full of golden dog fur.

'Raphael!' Sophie reprimanded. A golden retriever, tail wagging in high gear, retreated to the backseat. 'Sorry, Jonathan. She loves meeting new people. See that goofy, squinty, smiley look? That's her happy-to-meet-you face.'

I invited Raphael closer. She rested her head on the centre armrest and I threw my arm around her neck. Arthur's Pass! I couldn't wait to be there and breathe the air and feel the wind's breath — and the need to unload that brimming eagerness overwhelmed me. I was grateful to share with Raphael what I couldn't share with Sophie. It didn't take long to leave Christchurch behind.

In just under two hours we reached Arthur's Pass on State Highway 73, a winding and at times cliff-hugging two-lane road that connects Christchurch and the West Coast. I didn't talk much. I became too absorbed in the views. For being such a small country, New Zealand felt huge and endless. Green valleys unrolled for miles, dotted with sheep and their bleating spring lambs. Gray rock sentinels hugged hillsides. The snow-covered Southern Alps looked benign one moment and taunting the next. And the skies! The skies were so blue, so close that I could catch a handful and bring it home to Mom. An environmentally friendly souvenir.

In every vista I tried seeing through my father's eyes. In every vista I saw a new painting.

A cluster of white daisies grew at the roadside. I picked one and handed it to Sophie. She tucked it behind my ear. We stood on a gravel shoulder deep within Arthur's Pass — a ribbon-like cradle threading between towering and wild mountains. This was it. Sophie had found the same spot my father had once stood. This was *My Son's Inheritance.*

'I always knew I'd come to New Zealand.'

Sophie nodded. 'Part of your story's here.'

I took a deep breath and let the scenery fill my heart through my eyes.

A small bird flew by, singing, ringing like bells as it went.

'Holy cow!' I burst out, a sudden revelation exploding inside me.

Raphael bolted as far as the leash would allow, then sidled back, covering my hand in wet kisses.

'What's the matter?' Sophie asked.

'I get it!'

'What, Jonathan?'

'I've found him. He's here.' I made a sweeping gesture over the unfolding vista, a gesture that both presented the landscape and accepted it as part of my heritage.

Sophie smiled. 'You found what you came for.'

I almost didn't hear her say it, but she was right. 'He's still connected with Arthur's Pass and Governor's Bay and Akaroa because he *loved* New Zealand's landscapes. This land is what he wanted to give me — from one son of New Zealand to another — what he wanted me to claim as my inheritance.'

Sophie put her arm around my shoulders and didn't say a word, allowing me to revel in my discovery. And I didn't mind. Raphael whined and shot us a mournful glance. Sophie turned her face into the sunlight and laughed at Raphael.

There it was. The laugh I'd seen on her lips the very first day.

I laughed, too.

I no longer dreaded Thursday. Now, when welcoming the guests to 'William Stauss: His Art Was Life', as a representative of my father, I could speak to them about my dad with knowledge and understanding. I could also tell that grandma on Air New Zealand Flight 19 that she was right — that I didn't find my father in the cemetery where I had planned to go. I found my father in Arthur's Pass. Alive and well.

Notes on the Contributors

VIVIENNE BALL is a Wellington writer who has worked as a journalist and magazine editor. In writing her books, *Dipping into the Well* and *Peace*, she drew inspiration from the New Zealand environment and the hills and bush around Wellington where she loves to walk. She enjoys writing poetry and short stories based on her observations and experiences. She lives in the hills above Wellington and looks out on the changing Wellington harbour daily.

LINDA BENNETT is a South African-born, Wellington-based writer. She recently completed an MA in Creative Writing at the International Institute of Modern Letters at Victoria University, where she wrote a novel exploring faith, fundamentalism, love and psychedelic drugs in 1970s South Africa. An extract from this work appeared in *Turbine* 2013. When she's not writing, Linda works as a registered nurse and health advisor.

GAY BUCKINGHAM has been writing for a number of years. Her short fiction has been purchased by Radio New Zealand, *The Dominion Post* and *Takahe* magazine, won international recognition, and been published online. Her children's stories have been broadcast by Radio New Zealand. Gay has written a business history on commission, edited oral histories and most recently edited Sean Davison's *After We Said Goodbye*, sequel to *Before We say Goodbye*, the story of his assisting his terminally ill mother's death and the repercussions, published internationally by Penguin in 2012. A graduate of Otago University and usually domiciled in Dunedin, Gay has just completed an MA at the International Institute of Modern Letters at Victoria University and is currently working on a novel. www.gaybuckingham.co.nz

FRANCES CHERRY has had seven novels and three books of short stories published, as well as stories in various anthologies, school publications and on radio. She also runs writing workshops. After bringing up five children, she now lives with Ray the cat in Kilbirnie. More information is available at www.francescherry.co.nz

CELIA COYNE is a freelance writer and editor living in Christchurch. She has published two non-fiction books and is a member of the New Zealand Society of Authors. In her fiction writing she enjoys exploring unusual themes and using unconventional narrative styles. Her stories have appeared in *Takahe* magazine, *Penduline Press* and *Fusion*, a collection of speculative fiction (available at www.amazon.co.uk/Fusion-ebook/dp/B00A1BYR2U). She is currently working on a collection of short stories.

LILLA CSORGO is a Canadian who has made New Zealand her home with her Kiwi partner. Her plays include *Babes on Bay Street*, first produced at Toronto's renowned Theatre Passe Muraille in 1999. *Bangkok* was featured at RAW, a distinguished New York reading series, the On the Verge Festival (Canadian National Arts Centre), the Toronto Fringe Festival, as well as BATS Theatre in Wellington. *The Bigger World* was a finalist in the Canadian National Playwriting Competition and was part of the Groundswell Festival in Toronto. Two of her flash fiction stories were featured in the April 2014 issue of *North & South*. You can find out more about her and her work at www.lilla.ca

JANIS FREEGARD's fiction has been published in many journals and anthologies, including *Anomalous Press* (US, online), *Home: New Short Short Stories by New Zealand Writers* (Random House), *100 New Zealand Short Short Stories 4* (Tandem Press), *Landfall*, the *New Zealand Listener*, *Takahe*, *Brittle Star* (UK), *Cadenza* (UK), the *Momaya Press Annual Review* (UK), and *Harlem River Blues* (Fish Publishing, Ireland). Several of her stories have been broadcast on radio. She is a past winner of the BNZ Katherine Mansfield Award. Also a poet, Janis is the author of *The Continuing Adventures of Alice Spider* (Anomalous Press, US, 2013) and *Kingdom Animalia: the Escapades of Linnaeus* (Auckland University Press, 2011) and co-author of *AUP New Poets 3* (2008). She was born in South Shields in the UK and grew up in South Africa, Australia and New Zealand. She lives in Wellington and blogs at www.janisfreegard. com

ANAHERA GILDEA (Ngāti Raukawa ki te Tonga, Te Āti Awa, Kāi Tahu, Ngāi te Rangi) has written and published multiple short stories and poems. She lives in Wellington with her husband and child and is ever engaged in managing sand and juggling milk. She is currently completing her MA in Creative Writing at Victoria University and is working on her first novel.

VIVIENNE JOSEPH writes short stories, poetry and also works as a freelance editor, tutor and mentor. Her published children's books include picture books and novels. *The Leaping Place* is set at Mount Maunganui, a place she loves and one which never fails to inspire her. Her first book, *A Desirable Property*, won the 1985 First Book of Poetry Award. She was awarded an Honourable Mention in the 2001 UNESCO Prize for Children and Young People's Literature.

BRINDI JOY works as a writer and editor in the backpacking industry. She has lived in Seattle, Denver, New Orleans and now Christchurch where she now makes the most of the mountains and sea. Her work has appeared in *Landfall*, *JAAM*, *The Christchurch Press*, *Flash Frontier*, *Takahe*, *Wilderness* and *Backpacker Essentials*.

WES LEE is a Wellington poet and short-fiction writer. Her collection of short stories *Cowboy Genes* was published by Grist Books at the University of Huddersfield in March 2014 and launched at the Huddersfield Literature Festival. She has won a number of awards for her writing internationally and in New Zealand, including the

BNZ Katherine Mansfield Literary Award. Her writing has recently appeared in *Poetry London, Magma, New Writing Dundee, Riptide, Landfall, The Sleepers Almanac, Going Down Swinging, Hue & Cry*, and *Aesthetica Magazine's Creative Writing Annual 2014*. She has work forthcoming in *Westerly* and a suite of poems with *Blackmail Press*.

KATE MAHONY has an MA in Creative Writing from the International Institute of Modern Letters at Victoria University, Wellington. Her fiction has been published in *Best New Zealand Fiction Vol 6* (Random House), *Turbine, Takahe, The International Literary Quarterly, Tales for Canterbury* (Random Static), *Blackmail Press, Blue Fifth Review, Blue Crow Magazine*, and *4th Floor Literary Journal* (Whitireia). *A Good Person* was shortlisted for the BNZ Katherine Mansfield Award in 2008, *Jump, Jump, Jumping* (*Blue Fifth Review, Winter Quarterly, 2013*) was nominated for a Pushcart Prize, and *Freedom* was awarded second place in the *Takahe Literary Magazine* short story competition, 2014. She lives in Wellington where she is a freelance journalist and writing tutor.

RACHEL MARR – After trying her hand at illustration and fashion design, Rachel found the ideal outlet for her creative nature in writing. She is a mum to two daughters and fits in writing around running a busy household. She is hoping to publish a romance novel one day and perhaps a thriller or two.

DAVID MASON, at age eleven, was required to write a story that ended with 'and slowly sank beneath the waves'. He wrote about the sinking of the Bismarck which his teacher thought was pretty good. Now, a mere 53 years later, he's back with *Shine a Light*. Together with his wife, Janet, who also appears in these pages, he dabbles in ocean sailing and attempts to convey the romance and reality of this pastime in his blog www.yachtnavire.blogspot.com

KAY MEYER writes and paints by the shores of Wellington harbour. Both her parents were lively raconteurs but she owes her love of fiction to the many stories her father made up for her as a child, stories that, sadly, were never recorded. Kay didn't set out to write short fiction, but now that she's doing it, she finds the genre beguiling and challenging. The novel she's currently working on isn't the one she had in mind. She intends to stumble on with both short and longer fiction in the hope of further happy accidents.

WENDY MOORE now resides in the Wairarapa after returning to New Zealand in 2013. For 14 years she lived and worked in Europe, including Bratislava, where *Flower, Flowers* is set. Her short stories reflect a diversity of experiences in Europe as well as New Zealand.

DEBBIE NEWLOVE lives in Wellington, where she works as a psychologist. She was born and raised in Dunedin and has degrees from Otago and Victoria universities. Debbie is an enthusiastic reader of all types of fiction and in recent years attended the creative writing course provided through the Community Education Centre, Wellington. She is a member of a writing group and enjoys the supportive and stimulating environment it provides. Her short story *White Sunday* is set in Samoa.

JANET NIXON is a food enthusiast and sailing blogger who occasionally ventures into fiction. She lives with her husband on their yacht in downtown Wellington. Her food blog chronicles the gastronomic adventures of her fine-dining cooking club www.cookingclubwellington1.wordpress.com. Her sailing blog, www.yachtnavire.blogspot.com, is a narrative about a South Pacific journey that she and her husband made in 2010, to be continued when they set sail for Fiji in 2015. Janet is also a chef and lecturer.

MARGARET ORANGE studied with the NZ College of Pharmacy and qualified in 1952. She and her husband live in Masterton and have six children and nineteen grandchildren. Together, they wrote a collection of memoirs, published in book form, as a gift to each family member on their 50th wedding anniversary. Margaret belongs to the Blairlogie Writers' Group and to the Ruamahanga Probus Writing Group. She has had work published in *Tui Motu* and *Wel-Com* and was awarded second place in the Western Districts' Short Story Competition for her story *The Bay*.

HOLLY PAINTER is an MFA graduate of the University of Canterbury. Her fiction and poetry have been published in journals in New Zealand, Australia, and the US, including *Sport, Landfall, JAAM, Hue & Cry*, the *NZ Listener, Barrelhouse*, and *Cream City Review*. Another of Holly's short stories, *Jean*, will be representing New Zealand in *Everywhere Stories: Short Fiction From a Small Planet*, out this spring from Press 53. Visit Holly at hollypainter.com or in Singapore, where she currently lives with her wife.

LAWRENCE PATCHETT is the author of the short-story collection *I Got His Blood On Me: Frontier Tales* (VUP). In 2013 the book was awarded the NZSA Hubert Church Best First Book Award for Fiction. His work has also appeared in *Landfall, Sport, Dominion Post*, and *Hue & Cry*, and on Radio New Zealand. The short story *The Road to Tokomairiro* was the winner of the long section of the Long and Short of It Competition. Lawrence holds a PhD in Creative Writing from Victoria University and is currently working on a novel. He grew up in Canterbury but now lives on the Kāpiti Coast, and occasionally blogs about books at www.lawrencepatchett.com

BLAIR POLLY lives in Wellington. He has written three novels, the most recent of which is *Above High Tide,* a thriller set on the West Coast of New Zealand's beautiful and rugged South Island. He also writes interactive adventure fiction for readers nine years and older

(*Pirate Island, Lost in Lion Country* and *Sliders of Glass Mountain*) as well
as songs, short stories and the occasional blog post. More
information can be found at his website: www.blairpolly.com

DEB POTTER lives in Wellington and began her working life as a
journalist before moving into a career in statistics. She has written
children's stories and plays for teenagers and has a certificate in
children's literature from Christchurch College of Education (now
University of Canterbury). Deb also holds an MA in Creative Writing
from the International Institute of Modern Letters at Victoria
University. Deb publishes interactive fiction under the name of DM
Potter and owns The Fairytale Factory, a small Wellington-based
publishing company. Her books *Once Upon an Island* and *In the
Magician's House* integrate the classic pick-your-own-path style of
book with new e-reading technology. For more information, view her
website www.fairytalefactory.net

MAGGIE RAINEY-SMITH is a published novelist, poet, essayist,
short fiction, and flash fiction writer. She is also a regular book
reviewer on beattiesbookblog.blogspot.co.nz. She blogs at
www.acurioushalfhour.wordpress.com. For more information visit
her website at www.maggieraineysmith.com

JO RANDERSON, writer and theatre-maker, is recognised as one of
New Zealand's most original voices. Her writing is dark, funny,
poetic and absurd, and frequently peopled with outsiders, subversives
and dissenters. Jo's published works include short-story collections
The Spit Children and *The Keys to Hell.* Her plays such as *Fold, The Lead
Wait* and *The Unforgiven Harvest* are performed frequently in schools
and professional theatres. Her writing has won her the Robert Burns
Fellowship, an Arts Foundation New Generation Award and the
Bruce Mason Award as a playwright. She collaborates internationally
with visual artists, theatre makers and activists. Jo is also an acclaimed
performer, stand-up comedian, and exhibition curator (*My House*

Surrounded by a Thousand Suns). She is the founder and artistic director of Barbarian Productions theatre company. Please see www.barbarian.co.nz for more information.

KATHY SEWELL has written and produced several plays that have been performed in the Waikato. She belongs to the New Zealand Society of Authors and the International Writers Workshop. Sales of her children's book, *Haere Ra, Harry!* (Oceanbooks), have been steady and, according to Kathy, 'exciting'. Kathy has completed the Waiariki Creative Writing Course and will soon complete her BA in English and Media Skills at Massey University.

PAULA SLACK has had children's books (including educational) accepted for publication, as well as poems for adults and the occasional short story. 'It is a really nice feeling when your manuscript is accepted, for writing and reading are things I love to do — just like being out in the garden.'

BRIDGET L. STOCKER lives in Aro Valley, Wellington, with her partner Mattie and three cats, Louis, Oopsie and Karo. In 2008, Bridget was accepted into the Victoria University Iowa Creative Writing Workshop and was subsequently awarded a Creative New Zealand Mentor fellowship with Barbara Else (2008-2009). Bridget was then taken on board by Chris and Barbara Else of the TFS literary agency and, under their mentorship, completed her first novel. Bridget won the 2011 Royal Society of New Zealand Manhire Prize for Creative Science Writing (Fiction Category, 'Radium – A Love Story'), and was short-listed for the 2012 AUT University Creative Writing Competition ('Hotel de Garvey') and the 2013 Christine Cole Catley Short Story Award ('Terry'). She is still waiting for her first novel to be published and, in the meantime, is writing a second. Her profile can be viewed on The New Zealand Society of Authors webpage.

REBECCA STYLES lives in Wellington. She is writing a novel for her PhD project at Massey University. She completed the MA at the International Institute of Modern Letters (Victoria University NZ) in 2011. Rebecca has published short stories in New Zealand journals and anthologies, and blogs about New Zealand books at www.nzlit101.blogspot.co.nz